STORIES TO SHARE WITH MY PARTNER
BOOK 3

A BOOK OF STORIES TO ENJOY TOGETHER!

I0600990

By

J. F. NODAR

STORIES TO SHARE WITH MY PARTNER - BOOK 3

Copyright © José F. Nodar 2022

First published 2022

Published by Northport Booksellers

Email info@northportbooksellers.com.au

URL: http://www.northportbooksellers.com.au

Printed by Northport Booksellers Pty Ltd

STORIES TO SHARE WITH MY PARTNER - BOOK 3

Nodar, José

ISBN: [978-0-6453014-7-2] (print)

ISBN: [978-0-6453014-2-7] (Kindle)

ISBN: [978-0-6453014-8-9] (large print)

ISBN: [978-0-6453014-3-4] (ePub)

ISBN: [978-0-6453014-4-1] (audiobook)

About This Book

This book is an anthology of made-up short stories and may contain a few poems. These stories are an accumulation of weeks of sitting looking out the window and seeing life just flow into my life.

There is no rhyme or logical reason to the stories or their purpose other than to, hopefully, make you smile, enjoy them, and read them to your partner, child, or friends. You can also just pop them on your CD, phone or MP3 player and hear them in audio format.

They are short with each story taking less than four minutes to read, so in and out, I say and off to do other

ACKNOWLEDGEMENTS

Foremost, I wish to acknowledge the spiritual and moral support I received from my wife, Miriam V. Nodar. I dedicate this book to you, Red!

Without this support, and the many breakfasts, lunches, and dinners she has cooked for me in our twenty-odd years of marriage together. Without you, I would not have the strength to sit in front of a screen and pound the keys.

Second, I would like to thank all my readers for my weekly update and monthly newsletter and those readers that purchased my previous books, e-books, and audiobooks. Your feedback, insight and encouragement keep me going every day to sit, dream and pound the keys!

Finally, to all the authors in the writing trenches who have given me instruction, support, and courage to put pen to paper and help me this year.

Contents

TREASURE AWAITS

Remember when you were nine and someone said, 'treasure awaits.' Well, I do and you may not believe me, but if at the youthful age of seventy-nine, my best mate Artie said those same words to me for a second time in my life, treasure awaits!

There I was sitting on my favourite stool at the *Twelve Bells* pub in Northport when Artie walked in, slapped me on the back and softly whispered in my ear those words; treasure awaits!

Now, the words stirred something in my heart for as a much younger man, I ventured into many a place in search of treasure or opportunities but as age tacked on the years, I slowed down to where on many days just finding my glasses could be classified as treasure.

'Artie. Treasury awaits. What in the world are you talking about?'

Sitting down, Artie looks left, then right as if inspecting the entire pub to make sure no one could hear us. Besides Angus, the bartender at the other end of the bar watching the small television on the wall, there was not a soul around us.

'I heard that old man Barton over at the *Northport Shady Rest Home* has treasure hidden in his room. We need to visit him and 'acquire' his treasure. You in?'

'Old man Baron,' Artie says. 'Barton is eighty-one, just two years older than me, and Artie calls him an old man!'

'What are you talking about, Artie? What treasure?'

'Geez, Jimbo, you have not heard?'

My head bobbed up and down.

'Let me tell you what I heard,' and Artie scoots the barstool closer to me and starts telling me what he knows.

'Jimbo, during WWII, old man Barton was detailed to be a driver for an American General Smith. General Smith had the strange assignment of trying to collaborate with some of the strange misgivings that Adolf Hitler had about the supernatural.

Hitler instructed his Schutzstaffel, or SS, as we now commonly refer to it, to find these paranormal objects. The US Army then charged General Smith's unit to look for the same mystic items that Hitler believed could be used to further the war in favour of Nazi Germany. You heard about it. Didn't you, Artie?'

Again, I just bobbed my head.

'Hey Angus, how about a VB and put it on Jimbo's tab!'

Angus looks away from the television set, grabs a can of VB, slides it over the long counter to Artie, and returns to the mindless program on the telly.

Artie pulls the top off the can and almost gulps the entire beer in one go, but I can sense he left a little at the bottom to savour it later.

'No. No, I have not heard of Barton's military service or any special unit of the Schutzstaffel. What are you getting at, Artie?'

Artie smiles like a Cheshire cat, takes the last sip of his VB and slaps they can down and exclaims; 'He has Nazi gold hidden in his room over at the *Northport Shady Rest Home.*'

'Angus, another one and put it on Jimbo's tab.'

Angus twirls around like a ballet dancer and slides the second VB over to Artie, who again repeats his ritual and almost finishes the beer in one gulp.

'Artie, what do you mean he has Nazi gold hidden in his room? Have you seen it?'

'No Jimbo, but I heard from a friend of a friend of old man Barton that Barton mentioned this very fact to him, so it has to be true.'

'Artie, you know that there is a regular cleaning schedule at each private room at the *Northport Shady Rest Home* and there is no way Barton can hide gold and the cleaning crew does not find it. Goodness, even the nursing staff would see it. Maybe you misheard?'

'No, Jimbo, old man Barton has hidden it in plain sight, I was told, and now there is an opportunity for us to snatch it from him and off we sail into Fiji with the proceeds from the gold. Are you in?'

I think about this.

I never really like Barton before he went into the rest home. He used to come into the *Twelve Bells* and swaggers around like he owned the place. Hogging the pool table and flirting with Christy, Sue and the other ladies that frequented the pub on trivia night, so I really did not like him at all. Besides, while the Army pension is generous, it is difficult to live on $967.50 a fortnight these days, so taking these points into consideration, I gave Artie my answer.

'OK Artie, you convinced me. Now, how do we go about finding this treasure?'

With a big smile, Artie looks to Angus; 'Another VB Angus and put it on Jimbo's tab.'

Jimbo looks quickly to Angus and says: 'Hey, steady on Artie, I'm on a pension too, you know. This is the last one.'

'Well, I got a plan and it can work just splendidly with you now in. Let me explain.' as Artie picks up the can of VB that Angus had presented to him again and savours the beer.

'Thursday nights at the *Northport Shady Rest Home*, they hold a talent show and Barton is a regular participant doing what I have been told is his juggling act with some rubber balls. I propose we invite ourselves to the talent show and while old man Barton is doing his act, we slip out on any pretence and go into his room and find the Nazi gold. See, easy-peasy plan.'

'Your plan is to simply rummage around in his room until we find it? You do not know how much gold he has or where he has it hidden. Do you Artie?'

Slurring a bit, Artie answers me, 'Yes and no. It is in his room under a window ledge, but I do not know which window ledge.'

'So how do we pry open the window ledge? We will need to bring a crowbar or something, and I am sure they inspect packages when you go into a rest home these days. Do they not?'

'No Jimbo, this is not like airport security. There is no screening going on. We simply sign in; we give our first name and a false surname. We wear a large overcoat, for it is still chilly at night, where we hide the crowbar. We watch the show a bit, Wait for Barton to go on and then we mosey to his room and yes, each of us will have a crowbar and some gloves on as to leave no fingerprints behind, and we will 'jimmy' the wood out of the top of the window ledge until we find the right cavity with the gold. We stuff the gold in our pockets and we walk out and like the saying goes, Bob's your uncle.'

Well, it sounded simple enough to work, so I agreed to bring two crowbars and the next Thursday night, Artie and I showed up, signed in, watched the talent show, and waited for Barton to go on stage.

The moment arrives and as Barton starts his gig, Artie and I slip out and head to his room. We find the door unlocked and we slip in and each of us goes to one of the two window ledges and starts prying the top off ledges until we can see inside the cavity.

Nothing. Absolutely nothing inside the cavities but dust and spider webs.

We quickly put the crowbars back under our coats and return to the show to see old man Barton finishing his gig.

He was gleaming with a smile that almost lit the room when the spotlight hit him, and I swear he was looking straight at Artie and me.

After the show, Artie and I return to the *Twelve Bells* for a night cap.

'There is no treasure, nothing. All you heard was rumours. Now, if the police get involved, we might go to jail and have nothing to make up for it. What a mess you got us into.'

'I do not understand it, Jimbo. I am sure there is Nazi gold there. The stories have to be true. They must be true. How can old man Barton afford his stay at home? The military pension can not cover it alone. It has to be there.'

We sat at the bar drinking a few more drinks when we noticed old man Barton walking in and he went and sat right next to Artie.

'I see you boys came to see my show. I hope you enjoyed it.'

'Yes, we did.' I answered.

'Really? I saw you both sneak off right when I started my gig and just return right before I finished, so I wonder how much did you really enjoy it since you missed most of it. I am here because I am curious. Do you know who might have broken into my room and dismantle my windowsills?'

Artie almost screams at old man Barton, slapping his glass down, 'You bastard. I know you stole Nazi gold and have it hidden at home,' and storms out of the pub.

As we watch Artie leave, old man Barton turns around to me and again with the most gleaming smile, he says; There's my Nazi gold, and I'm takin' it with me when I go!'

Yes, treasure awaited, and it was all in gold fillings in old man Barton's teeth.

THE MIST

The mist drapes itself onto my boy scout uniform, making me feel damp, even smell. Whoever believed this would be a fun excursion had completely not thought this plan through. Why go camping in the Okefenokee swamp in February? What plausible reason would anyone come up with such a crazy idea?

Here we are troop 2537 from Travelers Roost Georgia near the Georgia and Florida border trekking in the misty dark towards, well, who knows where for the scout leader seems as lost as a ghost in a cemetery and the mist is so thick that I can barely see in front of me.

Suddenly, there is a tap on my shoulder. 'Bobbie, have you any idea where we are headed? Old man Thompson seems lost?'

'No Pauly, no idea and yes, I agree, old man Thompson seems lost and who would not be? You cannot even see the moon in this mist.'

'He is going to get us killed,' says Mikey, trailing behind Pauly and almost invisible in the mist.

'No, he will not get us killed, Mikey. Old man Thompson has been running troop 2537 for the past twenty-three years. My older brother Thomas was a member when he was my age and he told me some grand stories about old man Thompson. He said old man Thompson was always a barrel of fun to be with and many adventures would happen when they went camping. I am sure we are going to be fine.'

'I hope you are right Bobbie, for I tell you this place is giving me the creeps. Who thought of coming here, anyway?'

'I think our parents did,' said Pauly. 'I remember overhearing them when our last scout meeting was held back at the town hall in October. Remember Bobbie?'

'Yeah, I remember my parents all excited about it, saying it would be 'an educational trip' as well. Well, I do not think we will learn anything on this trip other than how to keep dry. Are you guys soaking wet as I am? It is getting to be a bit much.' I stated.

'You're right, Bobbie. I remember my mum saying something about this trip being educational but now I wonder if they had other ideas about the trip?' said Pauly.

'What do you mean?' Querying Mikey, slipping on a wet log.

'I don't know, Mikey. Maybe our parents paid old man Thompson to take us to this swamp and get us lost and we wind up being eaten by one of the many alligators that live in the Okefenokee. That is possible, right Bobbie?' Suggested Pauly.

'Will you just shut up? How can you think our parents want to get rid of us? My grandmother is always going on and on about how much joy I bring my parents. Does not your grandmother say the same about you?' I could barely see their nodding heads through the mist, but I got my point across.

'Now, just concentrate on where we are going in case old man Thompson is actually lost and we need to find our way back to the bus.'

'I am scared, Bobbie. I read that there are about a million alligators in this swamp and I am sure we are going to bump into one of them on this dark night. What is it anyway, fog?'

'Don't be stupid, Pauly. There are not a million alligators in the Okefenokee swamp. Didn't you hear old man Thompson explain that to us on the bus on the way over?. He said there are ten thousand to fifteen thousand alligators in the swamp. Not a million. You are such a doofus!' answered Mikey.

'Who are you calling a doofus? You dummy!' was the rapid comeback from Pauly.

'Both of you be quiet!' I almost screamed at them because I thought I had lost sight of old man Thompson for a moment, then I saw this large shadow standing about twenty feet in front of me.

'We will camp here for the night.'

That was it.

All this trekking into these woods and that is all; old man Thompson said as he dropped his knapsack and pointed in a circular motion for us to make camp.

'Oh, we are done for,' said Pauly. 'He wants us in a circle so he can corral us like a herd of cows. We are done for,'

'Bobbie, are we going to be, OK?' asks Mikey.

'Of course, we are.' I answer and yet normally old man Thompson made quite a commotion when selecting a campsite, and this time he was almost mysterious about it. As I looked at Pauly and Mikey, I saw the panic on their faces, and panic was now doing things in my mind.

'Now, guys. Old man Thompson knows what he is doing. He has been doing this for a long time. We are OK.' I said, sounding confident.

'Darn it Bobbie; I cannot see ten feet in front of me. For all you know, we might just be at the edge of the swamp and the alligators are going to eat us up,' said Pauly.

'He is right, Bobbie,' said Mikey.

'Where did old man Thompson go? Anyone sees him?'

We quickly turned around and scoped out the area; other than his knapsack, we could not see old man Thompson.

'I told you he is going to kill us,' said Pauly.

'Maybe an alligator got him?' Said Mikey.

Before I could answer, we heard a disembodied voice through the mist; 'You boys better hurry and make tent. It is getting late and we have a busy day ahead of us. I already made my tent and I am going to sleep. Hurry now.'

Without a word, Pauly, Mikey and I got our tents out of our knapsacks and pitched them quickly. and we made sure the tents were closer than normal, which gave us each a bit of reassurance that we should be OK during the night.

We each entered our little tents and went to sleep, only to be awakened by voices in the mist.

'Hey, guys! You hear those voices?' asks Mikey as he sticks his head out of the tent.

'Yeah,' answers Pauly. 'Do you think they are ghosts?'

'Come on guys; you are letting your imagination go wild here. It could be anything. Besides, it is still like pea soup, and you cannot see anything. Not even old man Thompson's tent and he has said nothing. So go back to sleep.' I tell them.

'You are right, Bobbie. It is nothing,' said Pauly.

'Yeah, nothing,' concurred Mikey.

And yet, as I laid in my tent, I did hear the voices.

Soft, high-pitched, whispering, but I could not make out what they were saying and to be honest, I did not think of finding out where the voices were, for nothing would get me to go out into this mist to investigate. My mind kept trying to decipher the voices, and they slowly faded away; before I knew it, I also faded into dreamland.

Morning arrived and with the mist gone, we got out of our tents and found old man Thompson standing close by speaking to a lady also in scout uniform who seemed quite agitated. and suddenly old man Thompson turns around and heads towards us, almost yelling.

'Listen up. We are pulling up camp and moving. We camped last night near a girl scout troop and we did not see them because of the mist and their scout leader did not trust us to behave. So, pack up pronto. Let's go, boys.'

That was it. The voices explained, No one was going to go missing or get eaten by an alligator. All the mist had done was plant us near a bunch of girls!

Well, my older brother said that old man Thompson was a lot of fun. Maybe he had done this before!

THE RED BUG

I could have named her anything. She goes by various names. For example, in Germany, she is called as a Bulli while in England, she is called a camper. In the United States, they refer to her as a bus; in Australia, everyone calls her a Kombi. My name for her is special, for she is my 'Red Bug.'

I fell in love with her when I was eighteen, but I could not afford her since I had just finished high school and decided which university I should continue my education, but life has a way of deciding for you sometimes.

In the summer of 1968, my parents invested in a restaurant in San Juan, Puerto Rico and so after high school, I headed there and never saw my Red Bug again.

My life as a restaurateur was interesting with long hours and meeting extremely exciting individuals. Despite this, I learned one thing: the restaurant business was not for me.

After two years at the restaurant, I broke the news to my parents that I was out of the family business and I flying back to her, uncertain that I would find her, for it had been so long since I last saw her. I was determined and while I knew the search would be difficult, I still left San Juan and heading back to her, my Red Bug, wherever she might be.

Through connections, I found a job which led me to banking an arena I never thought I find myself in. Not banking like at a branch during the day, which is what most people think when you say you work at a bank, but in the bowels of the institution, at night in the operations centre.

Here the machinery of the banking industry labours twenty-four hours a day, three hundred and sixty-five days a year, ensuring that payments go from account to account and making sure that debits equal credits. It opened my mind to a world of possibilities.

In this twilight world of cheques, I labour and continue to search for my Red Bug. Now that I was working full time, I had funds. All I had to do was to find her. Working at night gave me the opportunity to search the newspaper classified section and look for her. I did this every morning and returned to the bank each night to fulfill my obligations, but I always had her in my thoughts.

As luck would have it, I met a lady co-worker, and we hit it off. We enjoyed each other's company. Our interests were similar, and we felt at ease with each other so much that matrimony was a thought that we even spoke about and I was ready to do so that faithful Wednesday night.

On this incredibly special Wednesday night, we both had the night off and met for dinner in an outside café near the Peachtree Battle train station. Wanting everything to be perfect. I made sure that the reservation was for a nice, secluded table outside with plenty of fresh air and as little foot traffic as possible, thus ensuring no disruptions. The flowers (orchids, if you want to know) from a nearby flower shop arrived on time, just like I ordered, and the café staff made sure the flower vase was on our table, just waiting for us.

Arriving a bit early to ensure all was in place, I was pleased that the servers had dealt with all my requests splendidly. All I needed to do now was wait for her to arrive, enjoy our dinner and then propose to her right before dessert. I had the ring ready in my pocket and I felt nervous. I thought: Was this the right moment in my life?

She walks up to me and smiles and I can feel that the evening is going to be fantastic, romantic, and fulfilling. We order a few drinks, watch just a few pedestrians pass by, and smile a lot. Very few vehicles go by as well, for Wednesday nights are a slow night in the Peachtree Battle area, so I picked the café and the night. All is going as planned, I thought.

We finish our drinks and we order our meals and a second round of drinks. The night air is fresh, not cold.

The meal arrives, and it looks sumptuous, and we start and enjoy the delicacies we each had chosen for the night. My nervousness shows, and she asks me if anything is wrong. I answered nothing is wrong, took a sip of my drink, and smiled. She smiles back.

We finished our meals and looked at the dessert menu, which was my queue to get up and propose when I saw the first love of my life drive up and stop across the street from me.

There across the street is my Red Bug, as beautiful as ever.

I notice that a young man is getting ready to get out, so I excuse myself and rush over to him and as I get closer, I notice the 'For Sale' sign.

My Red Bug is for sale!

Without hesitation, I ask the young man how much he wants for her and he gives me the price. I do not know what to do. All my savings went into acquiring the engagement ring, $4,500. Gathering my courage and I show him the ring. I asked if he would accept the ring for my Red Bug. He laughs at me, but when I show him the sale slip and the price, he smiles and goes inside my Red Bug; he opens the glove compartment, takes out the registration papers, and signs the Red Bug over to me.

We shook hands and took the engagement ring; he went his merry way and I turned around and saw my date sitting on the table looking at me, flabbergasted at what was happening.

Returning to the table, I sit and explain to her what had transpired and how destiny had reunited me with my Red Bug. I explained my plans for the evening and what I had done showing her the keys. I was hoping for joy from her but received an ultimatum: 'It is me or that red monstrosity!'

As I drove home that night, I was happy I found my Red Bug.

WHEN THE FUTURE ARRIVES

It is so easy not to contemplate about the future; you know. You really do not think about it. Things like marriage, retiring and even death. The future is something that happens later when you assume you are ready for it. That is not the case these days. In the 2100s, things move rapidly, so you have to really start planning.

New parents enroll their children in their preferred schools weeks after they are born, never mind if the child is qualified or not. Everything now is connected, wired in, as some would say, and that happened with Mary Allison Bronston.

Mary was born on January 8, 2172, into a middle-class family in Spring Valley, Western Australia. At seven hours of age, the doctors at Royal Birthing Hospital imprinted Mary with all her family's particulars, including her family's social media standings and credit score reports, thus ensuring that Mary could, when achieving the age of one, apply to the school of her parents' choice.

Mary's parents did exactly that and enrolled Mary in the First Steps Learning Centre in Spring Valley and within minutes, her application was accepted, and Mary was now on her way into her future.

These early years were substantial in the development of Mary and in preparing her for her future career, which she would elect once she reached the age of twenty-four years of age. From those early days at the First Steps Learning Centre through her middle years of school at Primary School 2301 in Spring Valley, Mary's development moved apace. She showed she was a quick learner. Later, she excelled in high school at the respected Girls High Technology College. They then accepted Mary at the prestigious University of Technology of Western Australia. Mary achieved nothing but the highest scores at all levels.

From early writing skills to bio-genetic chemistry in high school to quantum mechanics while at the university, Mary was always the rave of her teachers, professors and the envy of her peers. Mary's accomplishments throughout life made her parents proud of her. From the moment she earned her 'first star' in the first grade to her 'merit award' while in the eighth grade and then graduating magna cum laude in high school and reaching the pinnacle of her glory as class valedictorian in her university class-the class of 2196. Mary then topped this by receiving many offers to positions in high-tech organisations like Meta, Alphabet, Moonlight Enterprises and Mars Industries.

One momentous day, after receiving a letter in the morning mail, Mary invited her parents into the living room. Her father put his arm around her mother's shoulder and pulled her close to quell their joint excitement.

'Mum, Dad,' she waved a letter about,

'Yes, dear,' answered her mum.

'I've decided on which job offer to take.'

Mary's parents could not control their excitement and her dad just blurted out: 'What organisation are you joining, sweetheart?'

'Mum, Dad, I decided that my career of choice would be scuba diving pizza delivery in Key West Florida for Peter and Glady Pancetta's Water Pizza franchise.'

When the future arrived, Mary was ready, but not in the way her parents hoped.

ANGEL INVESTORS GROUP

I am telling you; it is a sound investment. One of the best possible on God's green Earth. Why would you doubt me?' I query the small group attending my seminar on alternative investing strategies and options.

A small group of oddballs, really, if you think about it just by looking at them.

There is Sally Kitterman, retired librarian with forty years' experience overseeing individual requests from such banal situations as office space requirements for the local book club to finding a book on knitting.

Larry Stark is sitting next to Sally. Also retired, Larry is a veteran firefighter who has seen more human tragedy than I described in a book volume.

Next to Larry sits the 'professor.' Well, they call him the 'professor' because he simply has that look. Bill Ludlum just looks the part. He brings that confidence into a room by simply smiling and for thirty years, he was chief engineer at the Northport Sanitation Department. Yes, Bill collected Northport's garbage each week from the comfort of his air-conditioned vehicle and here he was sitting with us as if he was close friends with Elon Musk.

The small group has two other individuals—twins—Mary Liz Bennett and Elizabeth Marie Bennett, who proudly identify themselves as polar twins. Mary and Elizabeth took about thirty minutes (each introducing themselves to the group and explaining how they became polar twins. According to the sisters, it seems that when a woman's ovary releases an egg, the egg could split into two halves, the smaller of which is called a polar body. This egg now contains all the chromosomes necessary to join with a sperm to create a baby. But since it usually contains little cytoplasm or fluid, it's often too small to survive. It's possible, though, that a polar body could survive and be fertilized. Meanwhile, the larger half of the original egg could also be fertilized by separate sperm. The result according to the sisters: polar twins.

So here I am, 7 PM on a Wednesday night at the Northport Library, giving a lecture on potential opportunities in the private equity market, and all I could muster for an audience is this small group of potential misfits as investors.

After handing out the handbooks with all the research material and completing my PowerPoint presentation, I repeated my opening salvo: 'I am telling you; it is a sound investment. One of the best possible on God's green Earth. Why would you doubt me?'

Five somber, lost faces stare back at me.

'I got a question for you,' blurs out Bill Ludlum. 'How do I know that this investment is as safe as you make it sound?'

'Great question Bill,' retorts Sally, encouraging a bit of murmuring in the small group, and before I can answer, they threw another question into the mix.

'Yeah, how can you say it is safe? Are not all investments a gamble? Even these?' A smiling Larry Stark declares.

'I am not convinced,' says Sally, flipping the handbook back and forward as if the answer will fall from the pages and give everyone in the room the answer they want to hear.

In unison, Mary Liz and Elizabeth Marie state: 'We are not sure about the safety factors in this investment. Even the name of the fund is suspicious of us.'

I stand there dumbfounded. A perfectly presented PowerPoint presentation was for naught. Nothing I said made its way into the brains of these people.

'People, please settle down a bit. Let me see if I can answer your concerns one at a time.' I said in the most professional manner I could muster without losing my cool.

'First,' I point to the presentation, 'are there questions as to the investment philosophy that I bring to you tonight?'

Silence.

'You seem to agree with me that my approach to investing is solid and backed up with prudent sound advice?'

Heads nod to the positive.

'Excellent. I estimate the returns to be modest and in line with contemporary funds in the industry, while the expense is quite modest compared to other funds. Are we in agreement with these facts?'

Heads again nod to the positive.

'Your investment commitment has been explained, and it easily understood then?'

I see nothing but nodding heads in the affirmative for the third time.

'What else do I need to clarify for you tonight so we can move ahead with this investment opportunity?' I ask.

This time it was Elizabeth Marie that spoke first: 'These collections you are speaking about include a wide range of items. Rare wine collections, vintage cars, stamps and even baseball cards. This means that when we invest in these, we purchase and maintain physical items with the hope that the value of the assets will appreciate. We are hoping to get in when the price is low and right for investing and then we are in. Am I correct?'

'That is correct,' I answer. 'These investments may be more fun and interesting than other types, but they can be as risky as any other investment because of the inflated costs of acquisition during the bidding process. You also will not have any annual payoff, such as dividends or other income, until they're sold. Finally, additional costs are incurred with storage, insurance, and care of the items. What I bring to this opportunity is the skill required in collectibles investment, my experience. I am an expert and you can expect reasonable returns on your investment when you come on board.'

'We know all that,' says Bill Ludlum. 'We spoke amongst ourselves during our small coffee break. What we want to know can you guarantee they will accept us in the end?'

Now it was my turn to be dumbfounded, for I sensed I must have had a similar somber and lost face when I was asked this question.

'Bill, I am a bit confused by your question. What do you mean, can I guarantee they will accept you at the end?'

'Yes, that is correct,' chimes in Sally, and the twins nod. The professor is also looking straight at me for answers.

'Once you sign on the dotted line and transfer your funds, your participation into the Angel Investors Group is guaranteed; returns, however, are not guaranteed. This is where you invest and wait for your returns.' I gave my firm answer.

'So, there is no guarantee we will see the pearly gates when we die?' They said in unison.

'What are you talking about?' I exclaimed.

'The Angel Investors Group is not an investment company enabling humans to get into heaven?' Asks Mary Liz.

'No! The Angel Investors Group is an alternative investment company providing sound financial advice to help individuals retire and, once retired, to live off their investments. What could have possibly made you think I could guarantee you would get into heaven?' I spoke.

'Your name!' they all said, pointing to the PowerPoint presentation with the block letters clearly detailing the name of my company, Angel Investors Group.

As I left the library that night without a sale, I started thinking that, just maybe, I should diversify a bit in my approach to investing and maybe if folks are interested in getting into heaven, there might be a product I could sell. I might just call it religion.

THE PASS

Just wait until she is not looking.' Billy said as he continued spooning up the mashed potatoes into his spoon and dipping them into the gravy. While Billy did that, Michael, Bobby, and I kept our eyes on our own plates and continued eating our lunch.

Lunch today was just horrible. Mashed potatoes, peas and carrots, pièce de résistance, and calf liver. Why in God's Earth did the nuns think kids would like to eat calf's liver or peas and carrots, for that matter? Mashed potatoes were OK; I mean, French fries came from potatoes, so if someone thought that instead of frying them, they could be smashed up and made into a mushy and fluffy gobbledygook mess, why not go for it? Besides, the gravy you poured into the mashed potatoes made the entire effort all worthwhile. But the calves' liver-that had to be sacrilegious.

'Is she looking our way?' again Billy asked.

'No.' was the response emitting from Bobby's mouth as he continued to stuff himself with the peas and carrots. 'Sister Katherine is talking to Sister Beatrice over by the window, but she is awfully close to Martin's table. This will not work, I tell you. It will not work. Look at Sister Katherine-she is not smiling. She never smiles. That nun just does not know how to have fun. She has no sense of humour, I tell you.'

'Shut up Bobby. It is going to work. It has to work and who cares if Sister Katherine smiles, laughs or what not?' retorts Michael as he too stuffs his share of peas and carrots down. Looking over at Martin's table, Michael continues. 'Martin's table hates peas and carrots and they will trade us for the calf's liver. We just need to finish all our peas and carrots, swap our calves' liver for their peas and carrots, and we all win. Everyone concentrate and finish eating the peas and carrots on your plates.' Michael was adamant about the plan and how we were going to pass the God-awful calf's liver over to Martin's table and, in exchange, we were going to receive all their peas and carrots.

The plan was simple but brilliant. Michael had 'connections' in the kitchen. Albert was on kitchen duty the entire month and had heard that calf's liver was on the menu for today so Michael sprang into action as soon as he heard this bit of news and started canvassing the entire orphanage to see which table would exchange the calf's liver that day. It did not take long for Martin to approach Michael and agree to the exchange-peas and carrots for calf's liver, but fate has a way of making things go against the best plans.

For an unknown reason, the nuns changed the entire sitting chart for today's lunch. Instead of Martin's table been next to ours like, it has been for months, Sister Katherine moved Martin and his mates eight tables over and placed them next to the window overlooking the playground. This threw a monkey wrench into Michael's plan. Our table was now in 'creative mode,' for we needed a plan to counter this change of sitting arrangement.

'Just eat the peas and carrots. Mix them with the mashed potatoes if you have to and finish. We have to swap our calf's liver for their peas and carrots.' Michael said, and we ate as fast as we could. I glanced at Michael and saw him looking at Martin and exchanging glances.

Both nuns were still speaking and standing close to Martin's table.

I looked at the wall clock.

We had less than ten minutes to finish lunch before we were rushed into our afternoon chores. I looked at my plate and the only thing on the plate was, you guess it, the calf's liver. Looking around the table, everyone had finished and the only thing left on everyone's plate was the calf's liver and if by providence, we see Father Peter walk into the dining room and he hails both Sister Katherine and Sister Beatrice and the two nuns walk towards him.

'Now. This is our chance,' says Michael, who waves to Martin, and the exchange begins. Placing Michael's calf's liver on a paper napkin, we pass the liver from table to table and as if in a conga line movement, the entire room seems to sway to the movement as a small wave carrying the calf's liver goes from our table over to Martin's table.

The first cargo of the nasty liver arrives and is immediately replaced with a new napkin of peas and carrots and the process reverses itself and in less than one minute, the first load of peas and carrots arrives at our table.

Father Peter and the two nuns are in deep conversation, so our chance of getting caught seems slim, so the entire table is buoyed with this knowledge and we pass the second napkin of liver which arrives at its destination without an issue and we receive the second load of peas and carrots.

Two more exchanges, I think to myself. Michael is right. This is going to work. We only have two more liver napkins, and we are home free. Someone at Martin's table drops a fork and we see Sister Katherine turn and look that way. Everyone freezes.

'Simon, you need to be more careful. Get yourself a clean fork and place the one you dropped in the dishwashing pile.' Sternly Sister Katherine states.

Simon gets up and picks up the dropped fork but we notice he also gathers the rest of the peas, and carrots and places them all in one napkin and as he passes our table, he drops the napkin with all its green and orange vegetables next to Michael's plate as Simon heads over to pick up a new fork.

We are ready for him and have one napkin ready with one serving of liver and hand it to him on his return to his own table, but before we can wrap the last of the calf's liver, we hear Father Peter speak aloud: 'Boys. Let's hurry a bit. We need to finish and then go outside to do the afternoon chores. You have less than five minutes. So, finish up.'

Our table is now in panic. We have all the peas and carrots and that is not a problem for the chore of eating these vegetables will not be an issue. The issue is we have one last piece of calf liver and with Father Peter's announcement, Sister Katherine and Sister Beatrice are now walking around the tables to ensure the boys finished their lunch.

There are frantic looks between Michael and Martin. An agreement had been made and one half of the agreement, the peas, and carrots have been delivered and completely consumed. Only one last piece of calf's liver remains. There would not be enough time to exchange the last piece. Both Michael and Martin were now worried, and I could sense the pressure building in the room. If we did not finish our lunch, the sisters would ensure that everyone paid for the lack of appetite by providing extra chores. This was not good; I thought as I watched Michael just frozen, unable to act, sitting at our table. I had never seen him like this.

I am not sure what possessed me, but without thinking, I grabbed the last piece of calf's liver and, making sure Sister Katherine and Sister Beatrice were not looking, I stood up and threw the last piece of the liver over to Martin's table.

Unfortunately, baseball was never a sport I had done well in and I overthrew my mark and instead of getting the liver close to Martin's table, it went over their heads and landed, well splattered is a better description, all over the window high above Martin's table making a dreadful sound which caused Father Peter, Sister Katherine and Sister Beatrice to turn and see a flatten calf's liver slowly sliding down a windowpane.

This incident came to be known as 'the pass' and remained part of the lore at the Rayburn Boys Orphanage for many years and only spoken in fear for that afternoon both Michael and Martin's table spent the afternoon in the barn cleaning and shovelling, yep, cow manure while under the watchful eyes of Sister Katherine. I guess Sister Katherine had a sense of humour after all.

JERK

You know, Angus, this place is my haven, my safe harbour to which I can retreat and be myself without worries from the outside world. I am happy I found this spot so many months ago. How long have you had the establishment?'

'Well, my grandfather started the Grandville Pub back in 1895 and ran it successfully for many years. Then he passed it on to my father in the 1930s and he on to me in 1990 and I've had it all this time, but as you can see, times are tough and few come in these days. I'm glad you found the Grandville, though. You've shared some interesting stories.'

'I'm glad you have enjoyed our conversations; it seems I can bare my soul to you and I know you'll understand. How about another beer, Angus?'

'Whoa, you know you've seven already, and it is not even 1PM. Are you not pushing it today?'

'Nah Angus, there is really nothing out there for me today.'

'OK, as long as you say so.'

Angus pours another nice draft, and the ale's aroma seems to permeate throughout the pub. Suddenly the front door opens, sending in the blinding afternoon light and causing us to blink our eyes.

An extremely attractive woman walks in and slowly strolls toward the bar, her eyes darting left and right, casing the entire pub. She sits next to me and starts a conversation.

'Hi, what are you drinking?'

'I have Magic Beer,' I answer.

'Magic Beer? I never heard of it. Is it any good?'

'Yep,' was my answer as I lifted the beer mug to my lips.

'And why is it called Magic Beer?'

I take a quick sip of my beer and motion to the woman to follow me out the back door that leads to the alley. She stands next to me in the back alley and I say: 'This is why it's called Magic Beer,' I take off into the sky and do three quick rapid circles around the pub and land in front of her.

Without a word, I go back inside. I sit on my stool and take another sip of my beer as the woman stares at me.

'Wow, that's really amazing! I've seen that before. But I have a question?'

'Yeah, what is it?'

'Can you do that but from a higher height, say, the top of this building?'

Taking another big sip of my beer, I again moved to the woman to follow me and head to the back stairs. We go up four floors, open the fire escape door, and stand on the Grandville Pub roof.

Without a moment's hesitation, I run off the roof's ledge and again, circle the building three times and come back and land next to the woman, who is simply in awe.

Walking back downstairs, I hear her say, ' That was amazing,' 'Unbelievable,' 'Formidable.'

As I sit on my stool again, I sip my beer when the woman yells at Angus; 'Bring me one of these beers and bring my friend another one!'

Angus pours her the delicious beer and then slides another mug to me. I sip my beer as I notice the woman has simply gulped hers down and says: 'I'm going to try what you just did' She hurries to the rear door and we hear her running up the stairs and hear the fire door slam shut.

A few minutes pass and we hear a huge splat and what sounds like bones smashing to the ground.

Angus rushes out the front door and, after a minute or two, comes back in and returns behind the bar. Looking straight at me as I continue drinking my beer, he says; 'You know something?'

'What?' I say as I savour the last of my beer.

'You are quite a jerk when you are drunk, Superman!'

REVIEW

What do you think, sweetie? Do you think we should do it?'

'I do not know, darling; it is just a simple request; maybe we should. Hundreds do it every day and they are successful. Why should it not be the same for us?' I answered my wife.

'It is just, we have never done this before and they are asking for three reviews. What does that mean? How do we know what they mean by a review?'

'To be honest, I do not know. I never heard of this, but you know these days there are so many ways of getting to know people that this is another new method about which we do not know.'

'Well, to be honest, it is just too much. I mean, we are asking for acceptance of our request, and it is not like we are not willing to pay. We are not asking for anything for free. Right?'

'You are correct, darling, but people are a lot less trusting these days than when we were growing up. Everywhere you go, either in person or online, everyone is asking for more information about an individual before even answering a question. Just the other day, I found a new electricity provider online. I went to their website to find some information on their rates and guess what?'

'No, sweetie, tell me.'

'I could not find their pricing anywhere on their website. I found out that if I needed more information, I needed to provide my name, address and phone number and someone would contact me if they thought they could help me. Go figure. All I wanted was their prices, so I could compare against our current provider, but that is not the way this day. Just switch, that is what they say, just switch. No, I will not without finding out the rates first.' I sounded a bit frustrated, but I felt good saying it out loud.

'The world has gone mad,' I said.

My wife nods in agreement and says, 'I understand, sweetie. Just the other day, I was at the department store and I went to pay for a small purchase and they refused it. We do not take cash anymore. Just card transactions,' was the response I received.

'When I asked why I was told that this way, they can track all transactions to me and be able to help me in the future. Have you ever heard of something so ridiculous? How does that help me? I agree with your statement, dear. The world has indeed gone mad!'

'Well, sweetie, we need to decide. Do we provide this Airbnb host with one of our past reviews, or do we just stay at an alternative establishment like we have always done? What do you think?'

'Let's think about that. Why should we be put through a review, anyway? If there is a review to be made, we will do it about our stay, not the establishment about us. Is that OK with you, dear?'

'Of course. In this crazy world, we live in today, we need to make a stand. Agree?'

'Agree.'

'So, will you call your mother and tell her we are staying with her next week?'

'Of course, dear. She will not demand a previous review from us.'

'Excellent.'

'Indeed, dear, indeed!'

THE CHEATER

You know, Mariette, she cheats! How is it she wins so often and; besides, I saw her cheating! Yes, with my own eyes I saw her sleight of hand, cheating her way to a win!'

'Are you sure, Joe, darling? You could be mistaken. You know how your eyes are these days with cataracts. You might see things that might not be there.'

'Darn it, sweetheart, I tell you she was cheating, and I saw her. A bit of dexterity for such a young girl, but yes, it was not a mistake. She was cheating!'

'OK, now let's simmer down a bit and tell me, slowly and with as much detail, what you think you saw.'

'What I think I saw? I do not think! I know. I saw what I saw. A little cheater plotting at every game, scheming, would be a better word, in order to win at each round.'

'Yes, you said that several times but you have not explained what you saw, darling, so take a deep breath and tell me what you saw.'

I took a deep breath as Mariette suggested and calmed down a bit. I could sense a serenity coming over me, which would help me clearly describe this deceitful act perpetrated by this artful dodger. So, I detailed my wife with as many facts as possible so she could see that I caught the little deceiver in the act.

'At each end of each game, whether she wins or loses, it does not matter, the little scoundrel turns over the dominoes so they can be shuffled and I thought little about it but after four wins in a row, I thought I better inspect the shuffling of the dominoes and that is when I saw the deceiving manoeuvre she pulled every time.'

'Now Joe, just because she like shuffling the dominoes does not sound like cheating. You are supposed to turn over all the dominoes, shuffle them and then you get your seven pieces and start a new game. I see nothing that would show this as cheating. I am surprised by your allegations.'

'Yes, you are correct. At the end of each game, the process is to turn the dominoes over, shuffle them and then select seven new dominos to play with at the next game, but that is not how she cheats!'

'Well, tell me, how does she cheat, then?'

'Very smart, that little one she is. When she turns over the dominoes, she quickly selects all the doubles, you know, the double sixes, the double fives, etc. and then a few strategically selected dominoes of the same number of the doubles she picked and she wins each time. Clever little devil.'

'Joe, you know that all these offensive words you have used, such as cheater, schemer, scoundrel, little devil, are used to describe our granddaughter. Our sweet little granddaughter just celebrated her sixth birthday. Remember, it was your idea to gift her that same domino set from us for her birthday.'

'I do, sweetheart and I will finish this conversation by again saying she cheats and we need to tell our daughter as soon as possible.'

'And what do you want our daughter to do about it?'

'I do not know. You are her mother. You think of something and tell her to fix it.'

'Fix it? Our granddaughter is not broken. She is creative, I would say.'

'Creative, you say? Of course, you would say that. I never saw you cheat at Uno on the many occasions we play the game, so which side of the family does she get it from? His side? Right?'

'You know darling, if I did not know you, I would say you are impressed with our granddaughter and not offended that she has, let's say, a quick hand that she inherited from us. Am I right? And no, she does not get it from his side of the family either and how do you know I do not cheat in Uno? Maybe you have never caught me!'

Seeing her smile, I think for a moment about this statement my wife just made. Am

I impressed? Am I offended? Or am I disappointed that our granddaughter learned this sleight of hand all by herself and never asked us on how to do it?

'You know Mariette, you are correct. Our granddaughter is not a cheater or a schemer or any of those words I used to describe her. Let's say she is a magician who knows the power of the sleight of hand and uses said power to win and never gained talent from any side of the family. His family or our family. Agree?'

'Agree. Beautifully put, by the way. How about a game of Monopoly? Are you up to it?'

'Sure, as long as we don't invite our granddaughter.'

MURDER AT THE WRITER'S GROUP

The group stood there around the body, stunned at the congealed blood around Bert's head while small trickles of blood still dribbled from his head while his laptop and notebook laid next to his body under the table.

Not one member of the writer's group really liked Bert.

Bert was the sort of person who just alienated everyone. He was arrogant, full of himself. He believed he was more important than anyone else in the writer's group, patronising, overcritical, vain, and plain nasty. Why did the group tolerate him? Well, it came down to his critiquing skills, editorial prowess, and impeccable proofreading talent. Who would break his skull open and murder Bert? They all wondered as they continued standing around the body.

'OK, who is going to call the police?'
Mary says.

'Not me,' answers Bob, our Treasurer, 'whoever calls the police has to deal with them first and I do not want to do that. Besides, I always found Bert to be a patronising bastard. How about you, Felipe?'

'No, no, no, no. No way I am calling the police. One note from my voice and my accent comes through and I become suspect *numero uno*. Anyway, I never liked him. Bert was always super critical of my writing, saying it sounded too South American. Miriam should call. She is the most sensible one of all of us.'

'That will not happen. I will not be stuck in an extensive investigation. I have grandchildren to babysit for. Bert was always nasty to me and my short stories always said they were too feministic. I suggest Artie call. He is our group's Secretary and he should do it.'

'Wait one moment here. I just make notes of our meeting and that does not include handling the police, so I am not the one calling. Also, I did not like Bert at all. He was always correcting my meeting notes and making comments on my handwriting. If anyone should call, it should be Bill. He is the Vice President of the writer's group and now acting President since Bert cannot perform those duties. Bill, you need to make the call now,' and all the heads started bobbing up and down in affirmation of that statement.

I looked at the small group of contemporaries, all writers in different genres, and decided that there might be an alternative to calling the police.

'Guys, what if we solve Bert's murder first and then call the police? Based on our experiences as writers, we could do it. What do you think?'

'Are you mad?' states Mary. 'We do not know the first thing about how we to go doing a murder investigation. Well, at least not in real life.'

'Mary is right, Bill,' with a strong interjection, says Artie. 'We do not know how to carry out a murder investigation.'

Not to be left behind, Felipe also gives his *dose centavos* as he likes to say: 'Bill, just because you normally write about crime and murder does not mean you know what to do in a real-life situation.'

'I agree,' speaking up says Miriam. 'We do a little research when we do a crime story just to give the story a bit of pizazz and never get too technical. We would not know all the different intricacies of a true investigation.'

'That is correct,' says Bob, 'and we do not have any equipment or labs to analyse any clues. If we find any clues, it could be dangerous to arrive at the correct conclusion.

'Why do you mean dangerous?' asks Mary.

In a whisper, Bob looks at the group and says, 'One of us is the murderer?'

It was like a bomb had landed in the room. All stood there in shock and were surprised that Bob thought we could do this and if on cue, an uproar came out from all of the member's mouths.

'Bob, how can you say that?'

'Bob, what has possessed you to imply one of us could do this?'

'Where do you come off suggesting such an outlandish theory, Bob? You are crazy!'

And so on and so on. It went for a few minutes and I waited for the uproar to settle a bit and then I tried quieting down the members of the group.

'OK, everyone just needs to calm down. We need to be calm and come to an agreement on the best course of action. So, I propose we vote on our two options.'

'What two options?' asks Miriam.

'Our only two options, Miriam. I call the police as the group has suggested or we solve the murder by ourselves.'

Again, an uproar stirs up and a back and forth of questions, suggestions and implausible answers come out of the mouths of these four individuals.

Just as we continue to have our back and forth, Bert gets up and says: 'What the hell happened? One moment I am standing next to the table getting ready for our writing meeting and in the next instance, I am on the floor, bleeding and listening to you all making horrible statements about me.'

The group stood there opened-mouthed unable to utter a single word. Bert was not dead. He must have been setting up the table and hit his head when drop his writing book or something, hit his head and passed out. There was no murder. There was no need to call the police. A wave of relief came over the group.

Bert looks at us and starts a litany of statements all relating to each member's assertions about why they dislike him. Each individual member received a barrage of words too harsh to print and each left in single file out of the room. As I was leaving, Bert grabbed my arm and said, 'Bill, you are the only one who never spoke harshly about me. I feel that my time with this group is over and I will hand my written resignation to you shortly but accept my verbal resignation right now. I no longer wish to associate with such a group of individuals, but you, Bill, my friend, I can call you. Never said one bitter word about me and I thank you. I know you will do a wonderful job running the writers' group.'

Bert extends his hand and as I take it, I think to myself: 'Man, I should have whacked him harder on that big solid head of his.'

THE ESCAPE

Being placed in an orphanage is not a painless experience for an 11-year-old boy. Seeing the dormitory with over a hundred beds, all strategically placed in two rows, made for the young man an impressive vision.

What to expect, he did not know; whom to trust, he was not sure. He missed his parents, but he knew he could not be with them anymore; life had happened and there was nothing he could do but to 'toughen up' as the black-and-white TV westerns always say when the cowboy has a bad fall from his horse.

So, toughen up, he did. And a plan swirled in his head—escape.

He approached his fellow inmates and laid out his plot and plan for escape. There were enthusiastic expressions on their faces. He was making an impact, and he knew it and they agreed on a date and time.

As the day approached, however, he noticed some softening of their spirits. From twelve comrades, now only eight express their support. It was going to be hard, was their major concern.

On the day of the escape, only six conspirators of the orphanage show up to meet with the young leader. A discussion arises as to the complexity of the escape, and the young leader sees three heads lowered, knowing they knew they did not have it in them.

Then three remain, plus the young leader of the escape, but you could see that they too were wavering in their stance.

To the edge of the orphanage grounds, they trotted, not wanting to be spotted, and they reached the outermost corner of the property and stood. The decisive moment had arrived. Were they ready?

In the end, only the 11-year-old boy took off towards liberty, leaving the others behind looking at him as he ran, and then they walked back to the main building as if nothing had happened, enabling their friend, their new brother, José escape undetected.

Where he was going, he was not sure but escaped he did. No longer alone, for he had found strength and trust in himself.

STICKS AND STONES

As you get older, you realise a lot of things that, when you are young; you cannot see.

One of this these things is your parents.

Both of my parents are small—less than 155cm—and you would think I would have been about the same size as I grew, but I am full grown and only 99cm; way shorter.

This, of course, has caused me a lot of grief with my contemporaries and many of my neighbours.

They see Mum and Dad and then take a quick glance at me. You can almost miss me if I am standing behind either of them.

I am strong, have excellent skin colour, a wonderful temperament. Now I would go as far as saying docile, mostly. Add to this an early maturity coupled with high-performance capabilities and both a good fertility and longevity potential.

Finding a future mate, well, that is another story.

Having all these wonderful attributes, you would think that pursuing a mate would be easy, but it has not been.

Add to this the constant heckling, harassment, irritation, and annoyance of others because of my size, and my confidence is challenged if not confronted. Sometimes I just want to say really loud to them: 'Don't be such a cow!'

All this is because of a hereditary condition called hypo-heightism gene.

Hypo-heightism gene is a gene you inherit as a simple autosomal recessive trait.

This means that for a mammal to be affected by the disease, it must have two markers for the mutation (one from the mother and one from the dad). The folks that carry one marker for this mutation and one normal marker will be unaffected by the disease, but they can pass the mutation to their offspring.

So here I am, smaller than all my peers, because of this little imperfection that my parents passed on to me.

I suffered a lot because of this but realised that all this abuse, all these sticks and stones, do not harm me but make me strong.

Life is difficult, always is, and I am sure as I look out across the massive paddock, a pretty Hereford cow will find it in her heart to let me become a part of her.

UNDER THE HORIZON

My eyes linger on the horizon
A grey sculpture, a blur, it seems
Simmering in the sea
Thoughts turn to the mariners
They are spouses, fathers, mothers,
sons, and daughters
My mind focuses on the grey
structure.

I see someone that falls into the
sea
They struggle and strike at the
waves as if they can break them
They choke on the ocean water.

Now I do not see them as they
descend below
The grey sculpture also takes one
last bow

As it breaks after hitting the rock
ridge

I cannot bear to hear the desperate
screams of its occupants.

All lost now.

The ocean continues to embrace the
grey sculpture one last time

It is gone from view

Just under the horizon.

THE COAT

Autumn can be brisk in Northport, New South Wales and today was just typical for an autumn day as Brandon and I walked the river walk in downtown Northport on our way to lunch.

If you have ever been to Melbourne, Victoria and walked along the casino side of the river, that will paint you a picture of Northport, but we have no casino to spend our hard-earned money on the pokies or roulette tables. We have a very nice twelve-block long heritage country street filled with small store fronts lined along the river walk that combines your small stores like the local optometrist, *For Your Eyes Only Optical*, owned and operated by Dr. Frank Freeman and *Northport Dental Smiles*, part of a large Australia wide franchise and operated by its franchisee, Mark Osborne, A few doors down you find what has to be the premier hair salon in Northport, *Cut Me Crazy*, owned and operated by Albert Matthew Guzman, going on his sixteenth anniversary. A few stores south, you find an excellent antiquarian bookstore called *Village Books & Stuff*, one of my favourite stores to visit on days like today quickly, but that would not be the case this morning.

I lived in Northport all my life and have my small consulting practice in the Carmichael Arcade, which is right in the middle of this bustling little enclave. The consulting practice opened fifty-five years ago by my father and I now run it. Not to boast, but the water runs in my veins, as my father used to say. I lived on many ships with my father growing up and knew from an early start that this was going to be my life. After high school, I headed to Spain for studies and received a Diploma in Ship Surveying through the University of Cadiz and then completed a Master's in Oceanography and Marine Environmental Management at the University of Barcelona. I know my stuff in current marine issues, but I cannot be in two places at once. Hence my decision to bring Brandon to discuss a project I needed to subcontract to him.

Brandon's background is extensive. He has forty-five years in the marine industry. Eleven of those years, he managed a fleet of vessels for a construction company that operates, including many dredgers, tugs boats, small and large barges, multi-purpose construction vessels and many other work boats. When you think of the additional fifteen years in the oil industry working at a major refinery, maintaining its marine infrastructure, assisting with the berthing and sailing of tankers both alongside and at their moorings—vessel sizes ranging from 15K-430K, and conducting several ship-to-ship transfers. He also brought four years of marine maintenance on vessels of all sizes to his CV. A quite impressive curriculum vitae, if I say so myself and he looks pretty well preserved. I always tell people that salt air makes for a great complexion.

As we get near the restaurant, *Petite Maison*, one of the finest French eateries in all of Sydney, I get a text message and I stop to read it.

'Everything OK Patrick?'

I type the text response and answer Brandon; 'Yes. All good. Let's go in.'

The maître d greets us': 'Do you gentlemen prefer an indoor table or an outside table?' and before Brandon could answer, I say inside.

As we sit, the maître d' hands us our menus and we explore the extensive menu and fall into a trance just with the aromas coming out from the kitchen. Lunch will be great; I can just tell.

We place both our orders and drinks and get down to business, and then I see a pair of ladies sitting outside. They must have just come in right after us, and I could not help but point them out to Brandon.

They were stunning.

Both are dressed immaculately, not fancy, but nice, and the outfits they wore looked as if the designer was only thinking of them when he or she created the pattern. The younger one, a red head, looked fantastic in what looked like an easy-to-wear, A-line shape dress that flares out at the waist with a matching belt before falling just above the knee. Her shoulders gave the long sleeves a puffed shape, while I noticed that the notched neck gave her an immaculate finish. I nicknamed her 'Red.'

The other lady was older and I could not guess her age, but she was just as gorgeous and had short and cropped platinum hair. I dubbed her 'Silver.'

'Silver' was wearing a shimmery soutache trim dress, lending an endless beauty to each flutter sleeve on this sheath dress, making her a wonderful feast to the eyes.

'Why are they sitting outside?' Brandon states.

'No, sure. Maybe they wanted to enjoy the river view better or maybe wanted some privacy.'

'It is cold now. They do not even have coats. Look at them. They are both shivering,'

'Brandon,' I said, 'you are visiting from Jacksonville Florida and I am sure you are not used to wintry weather like we have here in our autumns. I would venture to say that these two ladies are natives and live in Northport by the look of them, so this weather, this little breeze, will not faze them. I am sure.'

'As you know Jacksonville's fall temperatures, I mean autumn, like you Australians say, average about 75 degrees Fahrenheit. What is that in Celsius, by the way?'

I needed to do a quick conversion in my mind, so I did it aloud for Brandon; 'Let's see. You start by taking the seventy-five and subtracting thirty-two from it. You then take that number, multiply by five, divide that number by nine, and produce an estimate of the temperature in Celsius. Brandon, your answer is 23 Celsius. The temperature in Jacksonville, Florida, in the fall, as you call it, is 23 Celsius.' I can sense a big smile on my face saying this.

'Still, with the breeze, it has to feel cooler. Why don't they just come in?'

'Not sure, Brandon but why don't we do something gallant?'

'Like what?'

'Let's go over and offer for them to sit with us or if they do not want that, maybe we offer them our coats.'

Brandon took a moment to think about that.

While Brandon took his time to ponder my suggestion, I thought I was dressed casual today, for I was wearing my old, well, I really mean old-fashioned, brown bomber jacket while Brandon had a grey pin-stripe wool business suit without a tie, so he was also sort of causal I would say. Brandon's answer interrupted my thoughts.

'Yes, let's go see if they would like to borrow our jackets. I am not game enough to ask them to join us. I am not as brave and adventurous as you,' Brandon stated.

'OK by me. Let's do it,' and we both go to the ladies' table.

We explained we saw them sitting there in the cold and that we would like to offer them our coats while they have their meals. They both nod and I give 'Red' my bomber jacket and Brandon gives 'Silver' his jacket and we point to where we are sitting and head back inside.

We notice they get their meals before us and soon afterwards, so do we. Brandon continues to smile at the table while we have our lunch and the ladies both smile and nod towards us.

As Brandon and I discuss the project I brought him down to Australia to work for me, the ladies show up and drop off our jackets.

'Red' gives me a warm smile and says, 'thank you' as she hands me my bomber jacket, while 'Silver,' smiles, and nods to Brandon.

As they leave *Petite Maison*, I can sense a sigh from Brandon.

'Now that was nice.'

'Yeah,' was Brandon's simple answer.

Concluding our lunch, we agreed that Brandon would go straight to the project and start implementing some suggestions we discussed while enjoying our lunch. I would return to the office to document our discussion to the client. As we put on our jackets to depart, I put my left hand in my pocket and found a piece of paper. I bring it out, open it, and see a phone number and 'Red's' name. I smile, show it to Brandon, and ask him to check his pocket.

Brandon repeats the same action with his jacket but comes up empty. No note with a number or name from 'Silver.'

'Oh well, back to the salt mines for me. You might just get lucky,' sadly, Brandon stated.

As we each go our way, I take out my mobile and make the call to the number on the paper.

'What happens? Brandon did not get a number!'

'Darling, Mother just did not like him. We will try someone else another time. See you home soon, sweetie.'

As I hang up, I smile, for I remember that on a remarkably similar cold and breezy autumn day, I offered my coat to my wife and looked at how we ended.

BOOK EM

'Harry, why did you decide to make this booking at this restaurant?' I ask as I bookmark my place in my notebook.

'Well Peter, I thought it would provide us with an excellent meal and enough privacy for us to conduct our conversation privately.'

'OK, Harry, what do you need to discuss?'

'Peter, my life is an open book. I have kept nothing from you in all the years we have known each other. Would you agree?'

'Yes, Harry, you have been open about your life with me all these years. So, what's up? Why all this secrecy in this, anyway?'

'Let me get to that. Let's order a drink,' as Harry waves the server over and we make our drink order.

Harry has a solemn face and I wonder what is troubling him, but I do not rush him. I have known Harry for many years. Back to grade school when we first met, he always had his head or nose for a book. As we headed to high school, Harry continued being the bookish type. Harry was always hitting the books. A bookworm you would call him, I guess, but a likeable bookworm. In my book, Harry has always been a straight shooter. Doing things by the book is his motto, so this impromptu luncheon meeting was really something surprising for him to do and I could sense an uneasiness about him.

I have always been able to understand Harry, but even long-time friends can have moments. You cannot really know what they have going on their minds. You cannot judge a book by its cover; Harry today was not himself. Today, he seemed tense, as if something were troubling him and needed to get off his chest. I was growing impatient with him so much I wanted to throw a book at him to jump start this conversation.

'Harry, what is troubling you? If I can help, please tell me. We have been friends for so long. In my book, we have no secrets, right?'

'Peter, I know what you do for a living.'

'Of course, you do, Harry. I am an accountant, you know that. I've been your accountant for years. What do you mean by that, anyway?'

'Peter, I know you are an accountant, but you are also a bookie. Do not deny it.'

'Well, that's one for the books. Do you think I am a bookie? Why don't you just accuse me of cooking the books while you are at it? You know that I have used every trick in the book to get you the best tax return from the Australian Tax Office. Have you ever seen me doing something off the books? No, of course, you have not.'

'Peter, there is no need for you to play the indignant victim as if you are taking a page from someone's book. I know what you do. It is a crime, and I am here to close the book on your operation today.'

As I get up from the table, three large Australian Police Force officers suddenly stand in front of me, stopping me. Harry gets up and looks straight at me, his best

friend of so many years. Then he says:
'Book em.'

PLAIN OLD
SATISFACTION

I'm totally distressed, Bob. I know I've muttered a bit to you about having some news to share with you last week and, boy, oh boy, I have a doozy to share. Thanks for meeting me here today for drinks.'

'OK Harry, just settled down. Take a deep breath and have a sip of the whiskey sour and settle back, relax, and just slowly tell me what has you so riled up.'

Harry takes a deep breath, well, several deep breaths, gulps down his whiskey sour, and waves to the server to bring him two more. My, oh my, he must have indeed a doozy to share with me, as he stated.

I've known Harry for over twenty-five years, since graduating from university at the NSW University of Technology. After graduating, Harry studied to be an electrical engineer and surprised his parents, his siblings, and his friends, especially me, by opening a publishing house for independent writers. Yes, good old Harry went into book publishing in a big way and founded Northport Booksellers.

Harry started slowly. He found a novice author, took her under his wing, went through all the steps necessary to nurture a successful author and before you knew it, he had a bestselling author that had over 100,000 books sold in the first year. After that, other novice authors and some established authors began knocking on his publishing door and success continued for Harry. Enough success that he slowly grew from a one-man shop to an entire group of thirty-five experts in the field from proofreaders to book cover designers to voice actors, all under one roof and all reporting to Harry for he kept his hand in the pot as they say.

The one thing that Harry did not do was his accounting. He hired a young university graduate to be the company's bookkeeper, and she was there from the beginning of his start- until one year ago. She was bright and was certainly professionally qualified and each month reported to Harry the company's balance sheet and everyone got paid. Harry was happy.

The server brings Harry his two whisky sours and Harry again just gulps down the first drink. He looks at me with a sad face and tells me what has happened.

'Bob, two months after my old bookkeeper left, I hired a new bookkeeper, but I noticed something was not right in just the first few months of his new hiring.'

'What did you notice, Harry?'

'The new bookkeeper was not presenting the same quality numbers as the previous bookkeeper. The numbers looked to lack clarity, confidence, visibility in the way they were presented before, so I brought in my accounting firm of Tatham, Black & Sanford (TBS) to provide some transparency into the numbers being presented by the new bookkeeper and provide a proper scrutiny of the business.'

'OK, Harry, you thought the new bookkeeper did not know his work and decided for an impromptu audit by your accountants. That happens quite a lot in the business world. What happened when TBS did their audit?'

'What happened, Bob? You ask, what happens? I will tell you. TBS came in, did some work, charged a handsome fee, and made some useful technical adjustments. TBS told me that our bookkeeper was intelligent, focused, and diligent. So, for six months, I went on my merry way, assuming that my financial data was fine.'

I was worried for Harry. He was now getting a bit agitated. 'Was it fine, Harry?'

'No Bob, it wasn't. I got the books reviewed by someone else other than TBS and it turned out that over AU$986,323.45 had been stolen. And who do you think did the stealing? Bob, who?'

Oh boy, I needed to tread gently. Whatever was bothering Harry really steamed him as he grasped his last whiskey sour in his hand.

'Damn, Harry, I don't know, but my only guess is your first bookkeeper. Who else had access to the company's funds besides you?'

'You are correct, Bob. It was she and a clever one at that.'

'How did she do it?'

'She created fake invoices, paid them, and pocketed the funds. Insignificant amounts for small proofreading projects through fake enquiries on our website. A remarkably simple but sophisticated fraud and not caught for so many years, hence the large number of funds embezzled and covered up. somehow the brilliant folks at TBS cannot see it in their so call audit.'

'Wow. How did you manage this, Harry? I mean once you found out?'

'Well Bob, naturally, I brought all this to TBS's attention and asked for compensation—after all, we also lost a huge amount of money in the time after their scrutiny was complete. After taking quite a while, TBS wrote to me to tell me they had done nothing wrong and offered me exactly nothing by as financial compensation. Bastards.'

'Again, wow. That was truly a poor response from such a large and prestigious firm as Tatham, Black & Sanford. What are you going to do?'

'It would be great to recover the missing money but I believe I'm not likely to get it from the bookkeeper since I assume all the stolen money is gone, never to be recovered, and she is sitting on a beach somewhere enjoying my hard-earned money. Instead, I decided I approach an attorney and see what I could get if I sued Tatham, Black & Sanford for fiduciary negligence or whatever the legal term is.'

'Did you meet with an attorney and sue Tatham, Black & Sanford?'

'Yes, Bob, I met with an attorney. She said that I could take court action against Tatham, Black & Sanford. She advised me I would expect to spend a substantial amount on legal costs. So, I have taken a different approach.'

'Harry, you will not do something dumb, are you?'

'No bob, relax. I am doing something simple and legal. I am going to tell the truth,' and Harry pulls a sheet of paper from his coat pocket and hands it to me.

A quick glance at the sheet of paper details just two sentences on it. The first one is a website address; www.TBSstandsforTotalBullShit.com.au and the second one is a link to a YouTube video—
https://www.youtube.com/watch?v=TBSZAZAP8Q.

'Harry, what is this?'

'The truth, Bob, the truth. I am just going to tell the truth and I did so by putting together a website and a YouTube video. They will simply tell the true story of what happened to me—and how Tatham, Black & Sanford handle their responsibility to me, their client.'

'What do you expect to gain from these actions, Harry? A public apology?'

'Well Bob, I hope that Tatham, Black & Sanford will be so ashamed by this terrible publicity that they offer me some form of compensation or agree to a fair binding arbitration process.'

'Harry, if this does not work, what will you get out at the end?'

'Bob, if nothing comes of this, I will at least have satisfaction. Plain old satisfaction!'

SO THAT IS WHEN THE FIGHT STARTED

I tell you, dad, I'm going to kill him!'

'Why are you saying that, Jessie? What has Jim done? Has he not brought home his pay pack this week? Has he spent it at the pokies? Has he gone and spent it on the ponies? What has he done to upset you so much?'

'What can say, Dad? He has done none of those things. Just worse!'

'Well, you tell me what Jim said and I will find him and pound him to the ground. No one hurts my little girl!'

'No Dad. I do not need your help with this. I can manage it myself. I do not want you to get involved. Do not tell Mum I am upset.'

Jessie just stood there in front of me with such a mopey face, sad eyes like a basset hound. I hated to see her this way, but there is only so much a father can do to help their child.

As I stood there, I thought of Jessie's wedding day. It was not an elaborate event. Jessie's mother and I had little, but we tried to offer her the best we could without getting deeper into debt. What father does not want the best wedding for his daughter?

As much as we could spend, we did, but wisely. My wife and I got up early and made hundreds of different finger sandwiches for the guests to enjoy. We made sure that we also had two beautiful flower arrangements at the church and upon completion of the church ceremony, I got my brother-in-law to get both vases and rush them to the reception hall in the church so we could strategically place them to make the dreary hall a bit more pleasant.

We did not stop there. My wife Louise is a wonderful dressmaker, and she made Jessie's wedding gown. It was not extravagant. The gown did not have a train, but it looked wonderful because Louise bought and used the finest material we could afford and it fitted Jessie beautifully. Jessie and Louise decided that instead of a veil, Jessie would have a floral crown made from the local blooming flowers and make sure the crown matched the two flower vases. When Jessie stood in at the alter—it was just magnificent to see her there.

'Dad? Are you with me? You were daydreaming?'

'Yes, Jessie, I am here. My mind just wondered away to your wedding day and my first thought was what could Jim have do to make you so mad?'

'He did nothing, Dad. We just had a fight, and I really got mad at him, so I stormed upstairs, got out a suitcase, packed it full of his things and came downstairs and plunked it right in front of him to see what he would do.'

'What did Jim do, Jessie?'

With a couple of tears in her eyes, my little girl explains, 'He picked up the suitcase and without a word, he turned and headed over to the front door to leave.'

'What did you do, Jessie? Did you say anything at that moment?'

'I was so mad at him I said a horrible thing to Jim.'

'What did you say to him?'

A little hesitant, Jessie waits a moment getting her composure and says to me: 'Dad, I said: Jim, I wish you die a slow and horrible death!'

'Oh, my goodness, Jessie. What did Jim do then?'

'Nothing!'

'Nothing. He did nothing. Did he say anything to you?'

'Yes, he did, Dad. It was horrendous.'

'What sweetie? What did Jim say?'

'So, you want me to stay?'

'That is when the fight really started, Daddy!'

THE KEY TO LOVE

Everyone looks for love

Is love like a key?

If it is, then my key to love,

Unlocks all the doors that are.

Doors locked within my heart.

It is also the key to life,

That unlocks all the doors that are

Some doors are locked within the
mind

Some are in my soul

That unlocks all the doors that are

Love is also the key to happiness,

It also unlocks all the doors that
are

Locked within my spirit.

The key to love,

Unlocks all.

FATHER WAS RIGHT

Pablo came from a family of gun-totters. His great grandfather was one, then his grandfather, then his father, and now he is one. A gun-totter.

Every village had one gun-totter family. In spring, the surrounding villages would gather to celebrate the season and all the families would visit another village. Here Pablo heard stories about the gun-totters. Fascinating stories the elders shared, but sometimes the stories were darker and solemn. The elders spoke quickly over those and seemed more interested in sharing the ones that mesmerised the young children visiting.

He never knew how they got the name of gun-totter and when he asked his father, all he got was 'I don't care. It pays the bills

Of course, that was not satisfactory to Pablo, so he did a little research and found a book in an old desolate building that had a large sign on top of the building partially destroyed: 'Nor*h*ort Libr***.'

He pored over the book but did not understand the symbols, scribbles to Pablo, but the book had something like heliographs and contained males holding pistols in their hands. This excited Pablo, who took his new treasure to his father and pointed the males in the heliographs to him and his father grunted, 'Yeah, they are gun-totters from the old days.'

OK, thought Pablo, now he knew there were gun-totters in the 'old days' for sure, just like his father. His great grandfather might be in one of these heliographs but as much as Pablo searched the book, none of the heliographs showed his great grandfather or any of his ancestors.

He earned his gun-totter title at thirteen, as most males do, and he began his training. It was a rigorous training that went on for ten hours a day, six days a week and continued for four years and each year, the training was more intense until he reached his eighteen-year when his father said he was ready for his first hunt.

Pablo was excited. He had heard many stories from other young gun-totters about their first hunt. The chase, the adventure, but none of the young storytellers ever went into specifics. When Pablo asked for more detail, they shrug him off or grab a mug of mushiness and drown themselves until they reach a full stupor. Not one young gun-totter share much, which made the hunt more exciting and worrisome to Pablo.

After a little thought, Pablo decided it was time to find out everything he could before his first hunt and went up to his father for answers.

'Father, do you believe I am ready for my first hunt?'

Jurgen looked at his young son and answered him; 'Yes. You are ready, my son.'

'Father, how do you know I am ready?'

Again, with a profoundly serious voice, Jurgen gives his answer: 'Pablo, you have spent countless days, years practicing your gun-totter skills. Do you feel you can assume your gun-totter duty and when a beast launches at you, shot, and not miss, thus killing it?'

'Yes, I tell you, father; I'm going to aim my gun-totter and kill it!'

Jurgen smirks a bit. 'What do you know of the beast, my son? What have the young gun-totters shared with you? Any details? Any information on what they faced on their first hunt?'

'No, father. All the young gun-totters brag but cannot provide much information about their first hunt, the few that have returned. Many do not return. That is correct, father?'

'Yes, many a young gun-totter has gone on his first hunt and not returned. Our family has trained well over the centuries and all of our males have become successful gun-totters and I feel you will also become one. Are you scared, son?'

Pablo looked at his father, unsure of how to answer. He indeed had trained all these years and as far as his gun-totter skills, he was one of the best. He could kill fast-running Rabbitohs, Panthera, from a distance of two hundred meters and these creatures were the size of a male, so he did not believe he fell in the category of scared.

'No, I am not scared, father. I am ready.'

'My son. Have you ever seen a beast?'

Now that was a strange question, Pablo thought. No one in the village had ever seen a beast, only the gun-totters that returned from their first hunt, and they spoke little about it. Pablo knew this much. The beasts were night creatures. He heard stories when he was a young boy about how fiendish they were, how ugly their faces were, how their devilish their black eyes looked and how dangerous they were, but no, he never had seen one. Pablo was happy he had not seen one, he thought as he looked at this father waiting for him to continue.

'Let me show you something,' says Jurgen, bringing out a heliograph and placing it in Pablo's hands.

'Tell me what, Pablo.'

Pablo sees a female, barefooted and loose-haired, wearing a dress. Her eyes did not seem on fire like the ones the young gun-totters told in their stories. Her skin did not look pale. She was beautiful. She had piercing green eyes that reminded him of his mother, Pablo thought.

'Who is this female, father?'

'That is the beast you will seek and kill.'

Pablo's mind exploded. How can this be true? How is this beautiful female a beast? There has to be a mistake; yes, that is it, it is a mistake.

'Father, I do not understand. Is this female a beast or not?'

'She is the beast you must kill. Tonight. Prepare yourself for the hunt,' and Jurgen left him standing there holding the heliograph of the beast he must kill.

How could he kill such a beautiful female? She cannot be a beast. There has to be a mistake, but his father had spoken and he would obey his father. He will do his duty for his family, for his village. Tonight will be his first hunt.

At the anointed time, Pablo met his father, who handed him a map pointing to the area the village people called the CBD and place an X on a building his father called a warehouse. Jurgen then spoke to him: 'Pablo. Do your duty tonight and return to us tonight with the head of the beast. Your family, your village, is depending on you to complete your first gun-totter quest!'

After a quick embrace, Pablo set off into the forest to head to the land of the CBD and find the strange warehouse building.

The trek took over three hours of arduous climbing and crossing small creeks. Along the way, Pablo saw artifacts that recalled his memories of stories he had heard from his grandfather and father when he was young. Burnt out machinery, discarded remnants of strange artifacts, many he did not recognise, but he kept on his mission, always checking his map for landmarks, and making sure he headed toward the building named the warehouse.

When Pablo reached the spot on the map, he recognised it. It looked like the object marked X on his map. Old, desolate, deteriorating, and yet he saw a fire inside. Creeping closer, his gun-totter in his holster, Pablo raised his head to see through a window what or who had made the fire.

Then he saw her. The beast.

The beast sat at a table and pulled a small rope gently toward her, but nothing was attached to the rope. The beast looked distracted and vulnerable, and Pablo kept low as he enters the warehouse; he hid behind a column. Pablo now had an excellent shot.

Pablo's finger materialized over the trigger, uncertain whether he could even stomach the idea of gun-tottering her. He had to. She was a beast, yet he could not bring himself to gun-totter her. But she is a beast who has killed people in his village and he was a gun-totter, trained just for this task. He aims and as he squeezes his gun-totter, the beast yanks on the rope and she pulls Pablo up with his left leg caught in a snare. He drops his gun-totter, and he dangles there upside down, helpless.

He feels something icy grasp his wrist. A hand.

Pablo is now staring into the eyes of the beautiful female. He had lost his gun-totter and was now at her mercy. She looks, seems to recognise Pablo and smiles.

Pablo was relieved because the female has beautiful intense green eyes, unlike the stories.

Pablo smiles at her.

The female grabs Pablo's head and gently turns his neck, and she lets out a chilling howl. and her fangs plunge deep into Pablo's neck and bite into it, hard, drawing blood that soaks the ground under Pablo.

Pablo is dazed. He failed. He would not be returning to his village tonight. He will never see his father again.

His story will never be passed on to his children and grandchildren, for it turned out that the beautiful female was indeed a beast.

Father was right, thought Pablo, as he saw the last light of night fade away.

MEMORIES ARE MADE OF THIS

In the early 2150s, Bartholomew loved to visit his grandparents, who lived in the quaint village of Little Burfordville, Section Eight in Devon, New Established England, close to the dried-up coast. At twelve, Bartholomew was too young to stay at home alone, so he accompanied his parents on their annual two-week holiday and stayed in a pod-and-breakfast near the remaining shores. Bartholomew's grandparents ran the Little Burfordville village shop for replacement parts for Androids and lived above the shop.

Bartholomew's grandparents knew their business. If you were looking for android replacement parts, their shop was the place to come to.

Need a smart AI module? They go it.

Need to replace the damaged, cracked, faulty touch face digitizer screen? Yes, they got it as well.

How about if you want to replace your old, damaged, or missing original internal documenting camera with new parts? This is your place as well.

On top of this, they carried an immense assortment of other necessary replacement parts on their website. Bartholomew's grandparents had been doing this for forty years now and they were the best.

Their village comprised small cement bunkers built after the war. On a small rise stood the large cemetery where ninety percent of the village was now buried. The few remaining bunkers faced the village centre where once large oak trees stood proud on the lush green grass, nothing but loose dirt now, and a small dry pond that used to be home to wild ducks, according to legend. There were no pavements or streetlights in the village. The only remaining remnants of the old legends were a red telephone box and the gun pillboxes.

Bartholomew's grandparents built their store in such a way that customers had to come through the front door, go through the security monitoring system and then they had to navigate the electromagnetic scanner to ensure no one was carrying an internal bomb. Even though Bartholomew was twelve, he had to go through this system each time he went into the store.

Bartholomew saw a timber floor during his first visit to his grandparent's shop. He asked his parents what it was, and they just shrugged and told him to ask his grandparents when he got a chance. When Bartholomew did, the answer was just fascinating. Timber came from trees, something that Bartholomew had never seen. He learned that in the old days, trees and plants gave off the oxygen humans needed to survive, but after the war and the evaporation of said oxygen, our new android bodies just did not need that chemical gas anymore.

Bartholomew always loved seeing his grandparents for two reasons. First, of course, they are his grandparents and second, the stories.

They shared with him stories about such wonderful things he has never seen. Open sacks containing potatoes, shelves filled with tins of peas, beans and carrots, packets of butter, salt, and custard powder.

Then some stories were even more incredible. Delicacies like soda pop, ice cream, Mars bars, Kit-Kats, Curly Wurley Bars, and you got to enjoy all these strange things in front of a fire!

Bartholomew's grandmother knew most of her customers personally and always stopped what she was doing to have a chat. Occasionally, Android strangers from other villages would come in and then the rumour mill would start, wondering who they were and what they were doing in the village. No Android could remain anonymous in such a small village.

Bartholomew loved to watch all the action. There was no currency, so no need for a till. Everyone had their universal token card to do their purchases. No matter what, Bartholomew still enjoyed going behind the counter, look under it and see an old till that didn't work but that his grandmother kept. She said it was for the memories.

His grandfather used to open the shop around midday and close late afternoon, which gave Bartholomew plenty of time to collect stories from his grandparents early in the morning and then watch them at work.

Right before dusk, his grandparents would go upstairs and settle in for the day and again relegate him with more stories of the golden days, as they also sometimes call them. That is why he adored coming to visit his grandparents.

To Bartholomew, it was a magical time when the gloom of dusk became covered by the vivid images in his mind.

Finally, in 2172, after his grandparents stopped functioning, the store closed, but Bartholomew never forgot his visits. He would travel back to the village, sit where the old oak trees used to be, and dream of the times he visited his grandparents' store.

IT'S HELL GETTING OLD

I'd like to make a missing report, please,' the aged woman addressed the young police constable standing behind the desk.

'When did you first observe this individual was missing?' he replies, as he takes a quick look at his watch, 7 AM, he sees; what a way to start the day, he thinks to himself. Constable Barker takes out a form, takes his pen out of his shirt pocket and looks at her.

'Heavens, no, no!' the woman stated. 'it's not a person who is missing. It's my youth.'

Constable Barker was unsure how to manage this situation, but he was the desk duty officer this morning, so he continued.

'May I have your name?'

'Alphia.'

Looking straight at her, he asked: 'Your surname as well, please.'

'Just Alphia. Like Madonna or Beyonce, you know.'

Constable Barker thought that his pay grade really did not compensate him for this type of encounter and brought in his sergeant and asked Alphia to sit by the wall on the bench while he spoke to his superior.

Alphia smiled, sat, and waited. While she did so, she contemplated whether she was doing the proper thing or just being finicky. Her daughter, Harmonia, was of no help when she approached her with her problem, saying the most over a used sentence in time: 'Whatever!'

Alphia did not agree with her. She was just fed up and weary of the changes she was experiencing and wanted it fixed. The problem was common and expected of humans, but not of her. Alphia is sure they can resolve the problem with good police work.

'Can I help you, Madam?' the Sargent enquired, standing behind the desk. Constable Barker stood next to the sergeant form ready and pen poised, waiting to take his first note.

Alphia groaned a little as she got up from the bench, approached the desk, and thought of how to describe her problem to these two men best. Would they even comprehend her dilemma?

'First, it is Miss,' and she relegated her problem. They listened attentively when she told how she woke up this morning and her youth has just disappeared. They asked some questions which Alphia just could not answer. She understood the question, but her memory just could not bring into focus the answer. Not only was her youth missing, but parts of her memory, she thought to herself.

The sergeant looked gobsmacked and Alphia saw the right side of his mouth curved a little. She was serious about this matter. After one hour of back and forward with both men, the sergeant said that he would need to refer her to someone with a bit more experience. It confounded Alphia when the sergeant said she best go down to the Northport Library and speak with Alessia Vassallo, the town librarian. Constable Barker was relieved that he did not have to complete a missing person form with this silliness and happily placed his pen back in his shirt pocket and smiled to himself as he saw the older woman leave the constabulary.

The town library was a short walk down from the constabulary and Alphia made good time, arriving just a few minutes after the library opened its doors at 8:30 AM. She headed straight to the counter and asked to speak with Alessia Vassallo. The clerk behind the counter picked up the phone, dialled, mumbled something that Alphia did not hear, and hung up. Alphia waited and then heard: 'How can I help you today?' Alessia asked Alphia.

'I am concerned that I lost my youth. I attempted to report it to the police, but they were of no help and suggested I come down to the library and ask for you. Can you help me?'

'I don't understand. Did you say you lost your youth? How can I be of help? Can you explain how you believe I can be of help?'

Alessia listened attentively as Alphia explained what she meant. Whether time had a 'hiccup' or something had happened scientifically that Alphia was unaware of, her beauty lasted an exceptionally long time. Why did she age overnight? Besides, the police officers said to come to her.

'Come with me, Alphia,' said Alessia. 'I have a room filled with books that might help you find the answer and one in particular.'

Alessia led Alphia to the back of the library, where many books contained shelves. It was devoid of people. Large tables laid idle waiting for someone to lay a book on them. Then Alessia stopped in front of a door, unlocked it, and led Alphia into a separate room.

In the room, Alphia could see rows of shelves along each wall, each labelled with a letter, starting with A on the top left-hand side. Alessia wheeled a worn timber ladder across the room, climbed it, reached for a book, and placed it on the single table in the room.

Alphia saw the title of the book: *'Aphrodite: The History of the Greek Goddess of Love'* by Charles Able River.

'This book should give you an answer to your questions, Alphia. I will leave you alone to read and I hope you find your answer.'

Alphia sat down and opened the book. She read for over an hour and studied the photographs. It was her in the book and she was young, healthy, and beautiful. Nothing like now. Old, pale and with all the aches and pains that are part of getting old as a human. She understood now. When she took human form and consorted with her mortal lover, Anchises, by whom she became the mother of Aeneas and the handsome youth Adonis, this was the chain reaction that precipitated her ageing.

Alphia opened to the page that showed her in her most beautiful drawing depicting her at the pinnacle of her beauty and looked straight into the drawing and prayed to her parents, Zeus, and Dione, to help her once again be young.

A fog suddenly descends in the room, engulfing it and Alphia, and as so as it appears, the fog disappears.

Alessia checks on Alphia during her lunch break and finds the room empty. The book is open, and it shows a drawing of a female, nude, standing next to a large vase, her hand draped over a shawl. The resemblance does not surprise her and reads the inscription: *'Aphrodite of Cnidus, Roman marble copy of Greek statue by Praxiteles, c. 350 BCE; in the Vatican Museum,'*

Alessia picks up the book, rolls the timber ladder into place, places the book back in its original spot, and leaves the room, locking the door.

Alessia smiled. She always liked her human name but was truly fond of her birth name that her father Cadmus gave her, Thyone.

It was a shame her grandmother had not only lost her youth but some of her memory, for she did not recognise her granddaughter, the daughter of Cadmus and Harmonia.

She thought it must be that affliction, dementia that afflicts so many humans, as

she returned to her office to catalogue
some new arrivals.

A LITTLE ROMANCE

She looked so beautiful from far away and I was certain that the closer I got to her beauty would not diminish but increase as my eyes gazed on her. From this distance, she was a larger creature than me, but that makes life interesting, doesn't it?

My strategy was simple: approach her and woo her from afar as to take precautions and not be mistaken for something else. Most of all, I am a lover and do not want to be mistaken for anything else.

There are many ways I attract females but over time I develop quite a unique method that rarely fails me. I am not bashful to share it here, for the reader might also try this method and increase his chances of romance. It's difficult to, so I gave this technique a name; 'rump shaking.'

As I step dearer to her parlour, I begin a spirited rump shaking. This shaking creates a sensation, a vibration that can be felt across the fibre of my entire body, transmitting like waves towards her and she feels the signals coursing towards her.

Closer and closer, I go in and she feels me. I stop. I advance further and pause again. Inching my way towards the love of my life, although she does not know she is yet.

I try distinct movements as I move closer. My pattern is exceptional and she can sense it. I am distinctly different from the others who approached her in shorter, more irregular movements, barely unique from one another. I am different. Unique. Special, and she knows it.

Imagine the daughter of Billy Ray Cyrus doing a 'twerk' and then you see me immediately and can tell how superior my approach is. My twerk is not only my rump but my abdomen as well, quite distinctive and, dare I say it, sexy!

My twerking causes vibrations that differ from the staccato, sporadic movements caused by the 'others,' inferior specimens, I would call them.

I made it a point to survive, enjoy myself as often as possible, and ensure that my vibrations' duration, frequency, and amplitude were so unique that she could tell I was someone else and mistake me. I did not want, what is the word used, ah. Yes, a man-eater, no, I wanted passion from her. For this beauty to be seduced by me and not for her to see me as something she could chew me up and spit me out, like the song by Cobra Starship's lyrics.

My presence gives off satisfactory vibes, good vibrations, you would say as I approach her and she knows it. I am positive she does. My vibration was quiet, for the extra quitter I was, the more successful my conquest was. The 'others' were too loud always and she determined right away that they would be aggressive and she fought them and won. That would not happen to me.

Suddenly she responds to me, twitches of her own, suggesting that a back-and-forth communication is achievable and for me to approach. I smile and she sees me glowing like the yellow sun, and I continue my approach.

I get excited as I approach her; she is behaving perfectly for me. A perfect mate, ready for me to take the spoils that I worked so hard for. Unexpectedly, I trip and make a sudden move. My most unusual vibration and her focus changes from 'Amore' to something else, fear, and she attacks me.

As she punctures me with her fangs and administers digestive enzymes into my corpse, I curse myself for being attracted to this black widow. The things we males do for a little romance.

WITH THIS SIMPLE GESTURE

I could describe Bill Walcott as your typical Aussie farmer. His cattle station is minor compared to some of his neighbours coming shy of four thousand square kilometres, but it keeps him out in the paddocks most of the day.

Today did not differ from any of the previous days, but Bill had worked up a big thirst and finished a bit earlier and headed to the local pub for a cold beer and chat with any of his neighbours who might have also finished early.

Bill sat on his four-wheeler and dialed his wife but got her voice mail instead, so he left her a voice message saying where he was going to be and even provided a time he might be home and for Miriam not to worry about dinner for him tonight and of course, if she had questions, to call him back.

Driving his four-wheeler to the nearest barn, he stores it, dusts off his Akubra hat, switches to his truck, and heads into town, arriving right after 5 PM, early enough to say he had a long day, which he had, and late enough for a nice cold one.

Walking in, he notices a lot of familiar faces and Bill returns all the salutations and notices that Jim Bartlett is sitting in a booth away from the main bar and joins him. While walking up to Bill, he motions to Angus, the barkeep for his usual and sits down.

'Hey Jim, you are all alone here. Piss anyone off lately and are hiding?'

'Hello mate. Yeah, I did. The missus is really mad at me for some silly thing I did, which I do not want to share, but yes, I pissed her off all right.'

OK, thought Bill, as he laid his hat on the table next to Jim's own Akubra. Jim was usually a very conversational bloke but if he did not want to talk, he would just sit with Jim and nurse his beer once Angus delivered it.

'Alright by me Jimbo. I can sit here, relax, and enjoy my middy,' and if my magic, Angus appears with Bill's glass of beer.

Bill raises his midday to Jim and mouths a 'Cheers' and sips the beer, savouring its sweet taste and the crispiness that it invokes in his mouth. After a long day in the dust, it is a fine way to complete the day.

A few minutes pass and Jim looks directly at Bill and says, 'If I share something with you, you will not blabber it around the town, not even your wife? It will be something between us. Right?'

With his most serious face, Bill just nods.

Jim takes a few minutes to figure out how to say what he is trying to share with Bill and after what seems like an eternity, he starts.

'Bill, we have known each other now for over thirty years, right?'

'Yes.'

'I feel I can trust you with what I am about to share with you, so don't make me come after you if I hear you told someone what I am about to share with you now. No one else knows this. Just Mary, me and now, you.'

Bill takes a gulp of his beer, expecting the worst news in the world from Jim, and again waves to Angus for a repeat.

'You know I love Mary, Bill. I am a one-man woman and have never fooled around on her, right?'

Bill just nods and just says: 'Go on.'

'Well, last night as I got into bed with Mary, I felt, well, frisky and even though I had a very hard day out with the cattle and had some issues with some hands and I was really wanting her but she said she was tired and of course I argued she could not be as tired as I was and of course that led to a big blue if you know what I mean.'

Just then, Angus delivers Bill his beer, and the conversation stops for a moment, but once Angus was closer to the bar, Bill responds.

'Jim, just look at us. We are not those young men that started collaborating with our fathers on our ranches. We have more years now, more aches and pains and we both had our wild times before we married so that once we found, in your case, Mary and in my case, my Miriam, we did not need to run around. So yes, Mary knows you love her but Mary also has the kids to take care of all the housework and she minds the business side of the ranch, right? So, she has a right to be as tired. Hell, even more tired than you, I believe.'

'Hell, yes Bill. You are correct and I did not treat her right last night and upset her when I said those things to her. Have you ever done that to Miriam?'

Bill takes a small sip of his beer and takes a moment to reflect and find the right way to answer his old friend.

'Jim, can I ask you a personal question?'

'Sure. What is it, Bill?'

'What kind of bed do you have, Jim?'

'What kind of bed? What do you mean, Bill?'

'Come on, Jim, you know, do you have a king-size bed, a queen-size bed, or what? That is what I mean.'

'Oh, we have a king-size bed. Why do you ask?'

Again, taking his time, Bill sips his beer and explains to Jim why the type of bed is important.

'Jim, Mary knows you love her. She also knows how hard our work is, not that hers is any easier. But when it comes to certain situations, sometimes a woman just ain't ready, and that happened to me about fifteen years ago and I found a solution and it has not failed me since.'

Now you could almost see Jim rise from his side of the booth. His interest perked up, knowing that Bill, while just five years older than himself, had a lot of worldly experience.

'Tell me, Bill, can you share your solution with me? I really want to make Mary happy and never endanger my marriage.'

'Of course, Jim. What are friends for? I can share with you this simple solution.'

'Hold up a second, Bill,' and Jim gets up, goes to the bar, and comes back with two schooners.

'OK, Bill, I am ready. Tell me this solution.'

'It really is simple, Jim. You get rid of your king size bed and get yourselves two twin beds.' and Bill takes a huge gulp of his schooner.

Jim looks at Bill in amazement.

'What do you mean by get rid of our king bed and get two twin beds? That cannot be the solution, Bill. It makes little sense.'

Bill finishes his schooner.

'Jim, right now, you get ready for bed and Mary might or might not be ready when you want to get frisky, as you call it. Correct?'

'Yeah, but how will a pair of twin beds solve my problem? How am I going to know that Mary has an interest?'

'Simple,' answers Bill.

'After you replace your king bed with the twin beds, you bring your hat into the bedroom with you.'

'What? What does that do? Bill, is this your simple solution?'

'Yes, Jim it is. You bring your hat into the bedroom and when you get into your twin bed and Mary gets into hers and you feel frisky, you toss her your hat.'

'That is the system? Does it work, Bill?'

'It does Jim.'

'How?'

'If Mary is not interested, she will toss your hat back, but if she is interested, Mary will bring your hat back and with this simple gesture, you both will be happy.'

BLACK SHEEP OF THE FAMILY

The afternoon sun had passed the midpoint in the paddock and some of the tree shadows were now bringing a little relief from the noon heat as the family gathered for a nice Sunday picnic.

It was nice to have the family get together like this. As Ralphie looked around, he could see Ella, his older sister, playing with his nephew Marky while his younger brother Ken was already hungry as always and was already picking at his food, disregarding the fact that it is polite to wait for all to eat together. Ralphie also spotted his other sister, Esme, relaxing under the shade, looking quite sedate.

To his left, Ralphie saw the Carmichael farm and saw that they also had picked the day perfect for a picnic and the family was out getting ready. Ralphie could see Emma and Evelyn. Emily and Elizabeth running around enjoying themselves but suddenly, his gaze stopped on another particular group in the grass.

He knew he was not a favourite of this group, for they always forsaken him and gave him a label he hates, but there really was not much Ralphie could do about it.

Close by to the females; Ralphie saw his cousins Rory, Finlay, Alastair, Avery, Balfour, and Barclay just laying in a group circle and having a hearty conversation.

Ralphie nonchalantly wandered closer so he could eavesdrop on the group and was shocked that by simply turning his head he could hear the conversation centred around him.

Rory: 'It was nice of the Carmichaels' to have this picnic today.'

Barclay: 'Yes. It turned out to be a perfect day.'

Finlay: 'There is food for all. No one will go hungry today.'

Avery was going to say something but stopped when he noticed Alastair was smiling, so he asked him: 'Alastair, what's the smile for?'

Alastair: 'I'm just thinking of Ralphie. How odd he always looks when we have one of these get together. Very odd indeed, that one.'

Balfour let out a loud laugh like an old goat's bleat. It sounded like that, probably because Balfour loved to mimic everyone around the station. 'Yes, he is odd. The oddest in the group. I do not understand how he is so unusual. No one else in the family is that strange.'

It hurt Ralphie's feelings when he heard the conversation. As always, he was being singled out in the family and made fun of. He hated being odd. Barclay interrupted his thoughts when he spoke out.

'Now listen guys, you need to stop picking on Ralphie or Mum is going to get upset with all of us and we may not take part in any future picnics or runs or anything else the family plans in the future. Let's agree that Ralphie's complexion makes him weird, but there is no need to constantly remind him of it. It cannot be easy for him.'

'Well, who made you chief consoler Barclay?' asks Finlay. 'Why do you care about Ralphie now? Is it because you saw him and your little sister Evie talking the other day?'

The group laughs at Finlay's taunt of Barclay and this gets Barclay all bother and you almost think he has a mad cow episode.

Barclay waited for the group to settle down before he spoke.

'Yeah, I saw Ralphie and Evie just talking, mind you, nothing else. So what? They can be friends if they want to. They know that is all they can be. Nothing else.'

Again, there was a murmuring in the group, but it died down quickly when Finlay blurs out: 'Lookie here. There is Ralphie leaning close to hear us. Hi, you funny thing!'

The group starts again in rambunctious laughter and Ralphie runs away toward a solitary tree in the middle of the paddock. He lays down under the tree and sulks.

'Why do they hate me so? I was born this way.'

'It's not my fault that because of a genetic flaw, my wool is black merino rather than white merino. Life is so unfair.'

As Ralphie lays under the tree, his thoughts wander off as he thinks of what possibilities could be in store for his life when he sees at a distance a dark point.

He gallops there and brakes.

Standing looking straight at him is the prettiest little thing he has ever seen. Evie is an ogre compared to this beauty.

'Hi. My name is Ralphie. I am a merino sheep.'

'Hey. My name is Evangelina. I am a Black Welsh sheep.'

'It is getting late. Mind if I walk you back, Evangelina?'

'No, that will be really nice, Ralphie.'

As Ralphie and Evangelina began strolling toward the hill for the night, he thought this might be just the start of a wonderful friendship.

Not bad for the black sheep in the family.

ON THE MENU

'Last call now. One more and I got to close up,' said Peter as he wiped down the bar counter for what he hoped would be his last time for the night.

There was only one patron left in the bar so Peter thought he should have just stepped up to the man at the bar and told him it was last call but for so many years he always shouted out the last call that it was just a force of habit that took over.

'Oh, that is OK. I will just finish this last bit and head off for work. Thanks for the offer, though,' he said as he sipped his drink.

'Off to work, eh? What line of work are you in that takes you out this late at night?'

'I am a vampire hunter.'

Peter just stares at the man and takes a bit more notice of him, something he should have done earlier in the night, but the bar had been crowded and Peter had been busy.

Peter thought the man was dressed odd but his attire looked expensive. He wore a tweed suit with matching gloves, which he had laid next to him on the bar counter on top of his black hat. Peter saw he also had a scarf with a pin and he also wore a tie that complemented the colour of his umbrella. Why would you even think you should colour coordinate your clothing to your umbrella?

His shirt was plain, but the man wore it well on his muscular body. Peter noticed that the man was tall compared to most of his patrons. Even sitting on the bar stool did not take away from his height.

'A vampire hunter, you say. Does the profession pay well?'

The man takes another sip of his drink and, looking at the few remnants of alcohol left in his glass, says: 'Yes, it does, but it can be tiring. I am thinking of taking in an apprentice. Do you know of anyone who might look for a job these days?'

Working at the *White Sheep* now for over three years, Peter has made a reasonable living. His monthly salary and the occasional tips have helped him maintain a good lifestyle but looking again at the exquisite attire of the man, vampire hunting is a more lucrative profession than bar tendering so Peter asks a few more questions of the man.

'Tell me, Sir, how profitable can the offer be for your new apprentice? The job market is pretty tight now with the economy booming as it is. What can you offer an aspiring apprentice vampire hunter?'

'First, my name is Percival B. Good, at your service. Well, the position has many benefits and….'

Peter interrupts: 'Wait. Your accent is not from here. You sound Canadian, right?'

'No. I am American born and bred.'

'OK, what brings you to New South Wales? There are no vampires in Northport that I heard of, anyway.'

'You are correct Mr…'

'Peter. Just call me Peter.'

'Great to meet you, Peter, and please call me Percival. I am in Northport because I have been tracking two particularly nasty vampires from Chicago, Aural and Lupe Smith, and all my data tells me they are here in Northport.'

'Chicago? They are vampires from Chicago named Smith here in Northport. Hah, who knew?'

'Technically Peter, their last name is Akeldama, but something quite infatuates them to the surname Smith, which I have not figured why, but that is not important.'

'OK, Percival, why did these two choose Chicago to begin with? What's in Chicago, anyway?'

'Peter, you might be interested in knowing that Chicago is at the top of the city ranking for the best conditions for these immortals. Chicago brings them the exact balance between cloud cover, many homes with basements and a rich supply of blood thanks to its large populace and outrageous amount of blood centres and blood donor drives. Add to this the wonderful restaurants, nightclubs, and bars that vampires love to frequent,' as Percival takes his last sip.

'Interesting Percival. Why did these two vampires come to Northport? Have you got any ideas?'

'No idea really, Peter. They were quite active in Chicago and then suddenly, they just left. I never could figure out why, but I tracked them here to Northport.'

Peter just stands there taking in the information and decides that one more question needs to be asked. 'Tell me, Percival, what is the starting salary for a vampire hunter apprentice?'

The man picks up a serviette, takes out a pen from his coat and writes on the serviette and passes it to Peter.

Picking up the napkin, Peter almost chokes at the number, looks at the man, looks back down at the piece of paper in his hand and just says: 'Seriously?'

'Yes. That is the starting salary for a vampire hunter apprentice. At least here in

Northport. Mind you; I pay in US dollars, so I am sure with the exchange rate, that amount would be a bit more. Do you know of someone who might be interested? Is that why you are asking?'

Peter has to make a quick decision. The money Percival wrote on the napkins was just unbelievable. It was almost five times what he made a year, and then he was going to explain the benefits, but he interrupted Percival before he could detail them. He needed to know more.

'Percival, my apologies. I interrupted you just as you were going to details some benefits of the apprenticeship.'

'Oh yes, I stopped mid-stream. Let me give you just a quick highlight. I really should write these down on a sheet of paper but there are: medical insurance, a 401-k, they have something like that here in Australia called a super, a phone allowance, a laptop, a car, and an expense account. The apprentice also has a daily per diem of $125 for meals. That's it.'

Peter had heard enough. This was an opportunity that anyone would grab, so he needed to be quick.

'Percival, could I apply to be your apprentice? I am not sure what the qualifications required are for an applicant, but I believe I can be quite a good trainee if you give me a chance.'

Percival stands up and looks at Peter standing behind the counter. Young seems in decent shape, not too bad looking, which will help with the female vampires. Requires a lot of work in the wardrobe department but seems curious. He is polite and asked some good questions, or so Percival thought.

Percival came from a family of vampire hunters. His great grandfather was one, then his grandfather, then his father, and now he is one. But Percival was a single man and in the last hundred years he could not find his true love, hence his looking for an apprentice to continue his family's legacy. This young man, Peter, might be just what he needs. Oh hell, what could go wrong?

'OK Peter. I will accept you as my apprentice. Can you start right now? Tonight, to be exact? For I am right on the tracks of Aural and Lupe and I do not want to lose them.'

'Yes, of course. All I need to do is close up and I am good to go.'

'Excellent. Let's go then.'

Peter takes Percival's glass and places it behind the counter. He then walks around the bar, heads toward the front door, locks it and gestures Percival to follow him to the backroom. 'We will go out the backdoor. It is a self-locking door and does not require a key.'

Peter motions to Percival to go first and as Percival walks past Peter, Percival feels a tremendous knock on his head and plunges to the floor of the backroom.

Gazed, Percival looks at Peter. 'Peter, what the hell?'

'Percival, you really have an attractive job offer, but I have decided not to take it. I received a better one just early this evening before you came into the bar.'

Suddenly, two silhouettes and Percival gasps from the shadows emerge: 'Aural and Lupe.'

As all three vampires feast on Percival's body, Lupe asks: 'Well Cousin, I guess we might stay in Australia for a while.'

'You should stay,' answers Peter, 'the weather is wonderful, the population is growing and they are quite naïve of our kind and are the most welcoming of new immigrants. Just don't tell the rest of the family.'

'You are right, Peter,' as Aural cleans himself off. 'There is no need to share this abundance of new, exotic blood. A smorgasbord of delights. Quite tasty, indeed.'

Peter smiles at his American cousins and says: 'It is a land where women roar and men thunder indeed! Help me clean up before the sun comes up. I got a big hen's party tomorrow night to take care of and who knows who will be on the menu.'

FREE BEER

How about another round, Bill?'

'Sure, why not Angus? And this one is on you.'

'No argument, there mate,' as Angus waves to Millicent behind the bar for two more glasses.

'Listen, this is my last one, Angus; the missus is going to kill me. It is after midnight and I got to work in the morning.'

'OK, Bill, this is the last one for tonight.'

Bill smiles, knowing the last beer is always the nicest.

'Great, but I am not leaving here until you tell me the story you told Tony last week. He said to me it was a true story about how he met his wife, but I did not believe it. So, Bill, I am all ears. Tell me the story and let me decide.'

Millicent overhears the conversation and tells the boys; 'Wait, you are the last two, so I am going to lock up and I also want to hear this love story as well. Go over that table and I will join you as soon as I can and bring you the last round.'

'Great mate. Will do,' says Bill as he heads for the table. 'I'm going to the loo, back in a second,' says Angus.

Bill sits at the table to wait for them and starts remembering.

Yes, he was looking for love but could not find the right individual, that woman that would be a superb partner, a good listener and an excellent friend. His friends suggested taking a trip, travel overseas, meet new people you never know. So, without thinking much about it, he booked himself on a tour group to Vietnam.

That was the first time he saw Munchie.

He was on the riverbanks of the Mekong River in the province of Can Tho Vietnam getting ready for a routine sightseeing trip and he saw her. Munchie, he gave her she that name the same day. She was munching on something and looked up at him as he waited for the boat to get ready. She stopped and came to him and just jumped on his lap where he was sitting. Bill was not really an animal person, but this cat was different. She had something, so he grabbed her and placed her on the boat as they shoved off.

Munchie had no issues being on the sightseeing boat as it leisurely travelled along the river with the guide pointing out the sights. Munchie even looked at the people in the boat, especially at the ladies, but Bill never thought much of it.

This routine goes for a couple more minutes when Munchie runs off and Bill chases her just to bump into an attractive woman also on the sightseeing boat from another tour group. It turned out and almost knocked her down.

Exchanging apologies, Bill sits next to her to make sure she is OK, and Munchie comes back and sits next to him, which startles the woman, but when Bill picks up Munchie, the lady relaxes, and a nice conversation begins between Bill and the attractive woman.

They seemed to get along just great when Munchie arches her back and bellows like a cat from hell and out of the blue, the boat hits a sand bank and tips overthrowing all the passengers into the river. During all this excitement and confusion, Bill somehow grabs Munchie, and he swims to the shore and so do all the passengers, but he never sees the lady again. She must have gone to the other side of the riverbank.

Everyone in the boat congratulated Bill for saving Munchie, but he wondered where the attractive woman was, but he never saw her again.

Weeks later, he experienced the second time that he met a woman with Munchie in toe. In the last week of his holiday in Vietnam, the heat was unbearable, and while Bill carried Munchie in his backpack, he had something to cool down.

He had heard of a local drink called cà phê cốt dừa which was a concoction that could do several things for you. I said that the coffee drink could be a pick-me-up, a fill-me-up, and a cool-me-down, all at once, and Bill was ready for it. He was also told the coffee blend was traditional drip coffee with coconut, fresh, and condensed milk. Then the concoction is spooned into a glass and served. It was like a fun tropical twist, kind of like a coffee cocktail, and when Bill found a poster with one displayed on it, he stopped for one.

As Bill waited for the coffee to be made, he took Munchie out of his backpack, rubbed her neck like she always liked, and looked around the café.

Busy was one word that came to mind, along with full. That is how the café was this scorching morning. The café is full of locals and tourists alike. When the coffee arrived looking marvellous, he asked for a small bowl and pour some for Munchie. Placing Munchie on the ground next to him, he watched as she enjoyed her share. Bill was not sure if coffee was good for a cat, but it was extremely hot, and Munchie just lapped it up.

A few minutes pass, and Bill savours his coffee when Munchie jumps on the table and begins bellowing. She arches her back and hisses loudly. Her action alarms Bill, but all he sees is a Vietnamese lady standing in front of him and motioning if she could sit next to him on the empty chair.

Bill places Munchie back on the ground, gets up and holds the chair for the lady to sit. She has a wonderful smile and, in broken English, starts speaking to Bill, asking him questions about his stay in Vietnam.

Before you know it, an hour passes, then two and they order lunch and then coffee.

As Bill is entranced with Bian, he found her name had a wonderful tone to it, and as the coffee arrives, Bill reaches out to hold Bian's hand, but Munchie hits the server's hands and the freshly mad cà phê cốt dừa spills all over Bian who jumps off her chair.

Bill quickly takes out his handkerchief, but it is not enough to clean the mess Munchie had created, and he tells her to wait that he will get something from the maître d'hôtel to clean her up and leave her standing there.

It takes just a minute or two for the maître d'hôtel to realise what happened, and he comes out to help, but Bian is not anywhere. She left, and all Bill had was Munchie sitting on Bian's chair, patiently waiting for him to return.

Grabbing the cat, Bill pays for the meal and looks down the street for Bian but no luck; she is not to be seen. 'Man, what luck? First the lady on the boat and now Bian,' Bill puts Munchie in his backpack and shrugs his shoulders as he hoists the bag over his back and starts walking back to his hotel.

Getting Munchie back to Australia was one big hassle involving a lot of paperwork and vaccinations against feline enteritis, rhinotracheitis and calicivirus. These vaccinations need to be valid through the quarantine period, which runs between ten to twenty days, but it was worth it because Bill always thought Munchie was special and she became quite a splendid companion.

Life was good for both Bill and Munchie. He left every morning for work, leaving her at home with plenty of food and water and each night, unlike most cats, she would wait for him by the front window to see his car pull up the driveway. Every time Bill saw her from his car, he would tell himself that Munchie was one special cat.

One of the first things Bill did after getting Munchie out of quarantine was he ordered her a special collar with her name and his address printed on it as well as his mobile phone in case Munchie got lost, which he always thought was a possibility even though she seldom left the house.

Being a cautious man proved to be a blessing, for as luck would have it, Munchie jumped over the back fence one night and disappeared for two days and nights.

Bill walked around the neighbourhood, left posters on trees and light poles offering a reward, but no one rang him. Maybe she got hit by a car? Thought Bill. Maybe animal control picked her up? If so, I should get a call soon, or so he hoped.

After two weeks, Bill felt that something had indeed happened to Munchie and he better accept that she was not returning home when his front doorbell rang.

Bill opens the door and sees a gorgeous woman in her mid-twenties holding Munchie in her arms.

'Hi,' she says, 'I believe this cutie belongs to you.'

'Yes, indeed she does, and thank you so much for finding her. I was looking for two weeks to no avail. Again, thank you so much.'

'My pleasure. I would have brought her sooner but somehow, she got her collar off, and I did not find it in the backyard until this morning when I saw all your information. Since you were close, I just drove up and returned her to you.'

'So, kind of you, please come in. May I offer you a coffee?'

'That would be lovely, and my name is Sally,' as she hands Munchie over to him.

'Nice to meet you, Sally. My name is Bill…. Well, you know that.'

'Yes, I do,' as she giggles to him.

As Bill places Munchie on the floor, Munchie rushes to the lounge and sits herself in the centre of it and watches Bill and Sally.

She is friendly and quite a conversationalist, and she takes Bill up quickly. As he walks the two coffees to the lounge, motioning to Sally to sit next to him, Munchie quickly arches her back, bellows loudly and jumps straight into Sally, who stumbles onto Bill, spilling the coffee all over herself.

'Why, this is one bitch-cat, Bill! She is mean. She just ruined my dress! Look at me!'

'Í am so sorry, Sally. I am not sure why she did that. Let me pay for the cleaning.'

'I am out of here. Damn bitch-cat,' and she heads for the front door, opens it and slams the door behind her without looking back at Bill.

Bill runs after Sally, but she is gone.

He is now pissed at Munchie and as he turns to give her a big scolding, Munchie is not there but a tall, dark-haired woman in her thirties in a long black gown.

'Hi Bill, my name is Minerva, and I have chosen you to be my mate.'

'What the hell? How did you get in here? Where is my cat?'

'Bill, I am she and I am also Minerva, Queen of Cats and I have been looking for my soulmate for the past three thousand years and I found you in Vietnam. Here I am now, just for you.'

'Wait a minute; you are Munchie? How is that even possible?'

'Anything is possible when you look for love, Bill, as I have and as I know you have.'

'This is not right. This is wild. You are telling me you can turn from a cat into a woman?'

'Yes, Bill, I can and back into a cat. Do you want to see it?'

'Yes, I would.'

Minerva waves her hands above her head and instantly she becomes Munchie, she rushes back to the lounge and with a slight purr, transforms herself back to Minerva.

Bill is stunned.

'Well Bill, how about you come and sit next to me and let's talk about us for a bit?'

Bill goes and sits next to Minerva and spends the next six hours conversing with her and sharing their lives stories.

Three months later, they married and are happy as peach.

'ÓK Bill, I locked up,' says Millicent, 'and here are the beers. Come on, Angus. Let Bill share with us his love story.'

Taking a sip of his beer, Bill starts his story for them.

'Well, I'll be damn. That is one hell of a yarn, Bill. Tony said it was good and it was very entertaining. True, I do not think so, but certainly worth spending a few dollars on a pint for you.'

'Agree,' said Millicent. 'These are in the house, Angus, so do not worry. I also enjoyed this farce. Now Bill, Angus, get out. It has been a long night.'

As Bill goes home, he wonders how lucky he is.

He is married to a wonderful woman and, to boot, who would have guessed at all the free beer he is getting by simply telling his true love story?

INVESTMENTS

I thought this night was going to be enormous for my career, so I might as well just dive into it and start the interview. 'Well, Mr Smith, tonight is the night. How do you rate your chances?'

Sitting in his large chair, Joe Smith, candidate for United States President in the year 2034, ponders this question as he swirls a glass filled with ice cubes and a two-finger dash of Zeppelin Bend Whiskey, enjoying the straightforward and rich whiskey before gathering his thoughts and engaging my question.

'Mr Leman, let me ask you a question first before answering yours. How long have you been a reporter for the *Financial World News*?'

'Mr Smith, well over ten years. Why do you ask?'

'Well Mr Leman, I grew up in Michigan and like my grandfather, father, and uncles, I have always been a union man working at the local steel mill until late in 1982 when I was laid off, along with over one hundred and fifty thousand other steel workers. I had just started at the mill and at nineteen, I had a young wife and a baby on the way. I had nothing to fall to.'

I watch as Mr Smith takes a sip of his whiskey and I wished I had one as well but knew better. Daring not to interrupt and I wait for the conversation to continue.

'Here I am, unemployed with a mortgage, a wife, and a baby on the way, so what do you think I decide to do, Mr Leman?'

'Please share, for I have not read or heard this in any of your previous interviews, Mr smith.'

'I went trap shooting at the local club.'

'Trap shooting, you say, Mr Smith. If I am correct, that is when you try to hit clay targets that are traveling away from the shooter at varying angles. Correct?'

'That is correct, sir and that is where I fell in love with the feel of a 12-gauge shotgun and the smell and the loud noise when the gun flares up as the bullet goes after its target. Quite exhilarating it was for me. Of course, this led to pheasant hunting, which brought a new sense of adventure for the hunt became quite thrilling now that prey was involved and I needed not only my skills with the shotgun but also my wits to engage the bird.'

'And this got you into politics. How?'

'Well, Mr Leman, little did I know that as I perfected my skills at the local trap shooting club, that destiny would bring into my life Mr Wayne Leach. We got to talking, then we went pheasant hunting and, over the weeks we spent getting to know each other, we could see that there was an affinity between us that crossed many aspects of our lives.'

Mr Smith motions to his assistant for another drink and continues his story as he waits for his drink.

'Wayne came from money and I was dirt poor, but we loved the same things. Guns, drink and having fun and somewhere in the mix of all of our conversations, politics came up.'

'From my research, Mr Leach was a stout Republican, and you have never professed any tendencies to either major party. That had to be quite an interesting conversation you both must have had over the trap shooting and pheasant hunting.'

Mr Smith nods, reaches for his drink, and nods to his assistant to bring him another one, even though he has just started the one in his hand.

'Our differences were our strengths and when an opportunity for county council came up, Mr Leach supported me not only financially but emotionally and before you knew it, I was representing the south constituency of my county.'

'This was just the beginning, correct?'

'Again, you are correct, Mr Leman. With Mr Leach as a mentor, not only did I succeed as a council member, but in just one year, I threw my name into the hat for the governorship of this fine state.'

'And you won. All seemed to go great, correct Mr Smith?'

'Yes, everything was going great. I won with a large popular vote. Made some great inwards into an antiquated school system and everything was simply perfect until….'

I knew this was the difficult part of the interview, so I gingerly stated: 'I know this part has to be difficult, but can you share with me your thoughts when you first heard what happened to Emily?'

Before he could answer the question, his assistant came with the second drink and placed it on the table in front of him. I could not help but notice that Mr Smith took a moment to wipe away a small tear he did not think I saw.

'The moment I got the call saying a madman had gone to Emily's school and shot three teachers and Emily and six of her classmates, the world seemed to have collapsed on me. I rushed to the scene, but there was really nothing I could have done. All were dead because a madman had a grudge against the school system, the same school system that I help improve. Instead of acting rationally and trying to bring his grievances to the school board, he buys an automatic weapon and snuffs out the lives of ten innocent human beings. All for a grievance that turned out to be a request to ban one book, and he was unsuccessful, so he thought he would remedy his grievance by committing murder.'

Mr Smith swallows his entire drink, takes the second drink from the table, gulps half of it down, and loudly slams the glass on the table. I look around and no one seems to notice, or if they did, disregarded it. I wait for Mr Smith to continue.

'You know, Mr Leman, that moment galvanised me. It made me realise that I could not fix one state. I needed to fix the entire country, so I embarked on a mission to run for President of the United States and here we are in 2034 at the youthful age of seventy-one. If I win, I will accomplish my mission.'

'Mr Smith, your campaign centred on the US Constitution's second amendment and how you would make it right for everyone. How do you plan to do this? Is this something you can share with me today right before the major networks plaster tonight's results all over the television screens?' I asked, hoping to get the scoop of a lifetime.

'Mr Leman, the second amendment of the US constitution, reads: *"A well-regulated Militia, being necessary to the security of a free State, the right of the people to keep and bear Arms, shall not be infringed."* How do you interpret this today, two-hundred and forty-three years after they adopted it in 1791?'

This sudden turn of events took me aback a bit. Instead of me doing the questions, suddenly, I am asked to answer one. I took a moment to reflect and then answered the question asked by, potentially, the 49th President of the United States.

'Mr Smith, I have to answer your question from a personal point of view. I know fully that in the U. S. Supreme Court case in the 2008 landmark case *District of Columbia v. Heller*, the Court concluded that the Second Amendment includes the right of individuals to bear arms for self-defence and I agree with this controversial decision.'

'So, Mr Leman, you are then part of a "well-regulated militia" in your state?'

'Mr Smith, as of 2010, 23 states and territories maintained their own State Defense Force (SDFs). These forces, unlike federal organizations, such as the National Guard, are under the sole authority of state or territorial governments and cannot be commanded by the federal government, but I do not belong to any militia to answer your question.'

'I see,' states Mr Smith with a smile on his face as he sips his whiskey. 'So, the Public Safety and Recreational Firearms Use Protection Act of 1994, which banned private use of assault weapons, such as certain semiautomatic rifles, which I know you know expired in 2004 and Congress refused to reinstall the ban which allowed madmen like the one that killed my Emily to buy these machine guns, which seems OK to you. Tell me if this is what you are saying.'

Sensing a terrible confrontation might erupt, I decide to deescalate the conversion by turning it around.

'Mr Smith, your entire campaign for election as the next President of the United States was to support the second amendment, the right to bear arms. Why do I sense a change in your attitude now?'

'No, Mr Leman, there is no change in my position on the second amendment. If I am elected, I propose to ensure that everyone follows this amendment, just like they did in 1791.'

'What a relief Mr Smith; I thought you were going to revoke the amendment and take away the right to bear arms.' I said with relief in my voice.

Getting up Mr Smith again smiles at me and says: 'No Mr Leman, I will one-hundred percent support the literal meaning of the second amendment as it was written in 1791 and I will make sure that all weapons are removed from each household in America and replaced with single flint muskets just like they had in 1791.'

I stood up. My mind was going wild at this statement.

'Mr Smith, what happens if the Russians invade us? They will find a disarmed America. How do we defend ourselves?'

'Mr Leman, there is nothing to worry with the Russians. If the Ukrainians could defeat them back in 2023, we will have no problem with them in 2034. Have a good night. I need to get ready for my victory speech.'

As Mr Smith leaves me standing in the room, I wonder if I should start reviewing my investment portfolio and start looking for a musket-making company to invest in.

CAREER CHOICES

How does it feel to have won the 2092 World Series?' I ask José Fernando Ramírez as he basks in his glory after not only winning the World Series in four games but pitching a perfect game, no runs, no hits, twenty-one strikeouts and hitting the one home run to win the last game.

'Well, Mr Leman, what can I say? I'm going to Disneyland is inappropriate since the place is underwater these days due to all the global warming but I am thrilled to have taken the Kangaroo Giants to their first world championship.'

'Tell me José, how does your family feel about this?'

José takes a few moments before answering.

'Mr Leman, my family is just as thrilled as I am. My older brother Miguel was going to be a pitcher himself but as smart as he was as a young boy to this day, we do not know why he put his hand in the paper shredder that morning of April 15th, 2083, and destroyed his chances for pitching in the world league.'

'Yes, it was a terrible accident to Miguel. That is when you started the sport yourself?'

'Yes, Mr Leman, it was. As a young boy, I was not great at many activities. I was always a happy child enjoying friendships and was well-liked by all the other children, but I lacked the talents of my siblings. Of course, my parents were worried. They took me to multiple medical doctors, psychologists, and other child development experts.'

'Did they come up with an answer for you, José?'

'Nothing. Nada. Zip. The specialists were stumped, so my parents gave up because the medical bills back them were enormous, not like today thanks to the Universal Medical Plans.'

'How did your older sister, Maria, help you along with your career, José?'

'Ah Maria, the best sister any man would want. She sings. She dances. She taught herself aerobic dancing and now is a prima ballerina assoluta for the Mars International Ballet Company on Mars City. Have you seen her in Hypanis Valles Swan River? She is just beautiful as she performs this modern version of that old classic Swan Lake.'

'No, I have not travelled out worldly this year. I will do so next year and catch her show. Let me ask you something a bit more personal if I may, José?'

'Of course, Mr Leman, my life is an open tablet.'

'What can you share, José, about the first time you notice you were special?'

'Oh, there is really nothing special to tell, really. One day, while playing with Miguel and his friends in the park, I spotted two tiny little bugs with different spots. I ran to my Mama to show her but she could not see any spots at all and just told me to keep playing with Miguel, which I did. I was playing right-fielder and Miguel was the pitcher, so I could not show him the bugs until the inning was finished. Miguel tried to see the spots in the two bugs but said he could see nothing and for me to put the little things down, for it was time for me to get ready for my first time up to bat.'

'So, this is when you got your first lesson at batting, correct, José?'

'it was indeed my first lesson, Mr Leman. Miguel told me that normally the pitcher batted last but no one minded if I went last because it gave me more time to see what they did. Miguel did his best to explain and point out things to me, but I really failed to understand his frustrating explanations.'

'Why were they frustrating to you, José?'

'I did not see what the big thing was. What was so difficult in hitting that enormous ball?' I told Miguel.

'Wait, you said you saw a big ball?'

'Yes, I did, Mr Leman. Let me finish the story.'

'Please continue José, apologies for the interruption.'

'I walked to the home plate, well I swagger because that was what all the older boys did and waited for the pitcher to throw me the ball. The first pitch was outside, and I didn't bother to swing. The second pitch was low, and I skipped that one too. The third pitch was a fastball down the middle which I could not resist and took a casual swing and hit it over the shortstop's head for a solid hit and got a triple out of it.'

'That was your first hit ever?'

'Yes, it was. It felt great. Miguel batted next and got me to home plate and the spectators went wild for we won our game with that hit.'

'Do you think it was a lucky swing, José?'

'No, Mr Leman, it was not. On the way home, Miguel and I sat in the back seat of our dad's 2069 Tesla Y and he asked me how'd I did that. I replied it was impossible to miss something as big as a beach ball and the way it was spinning. I figured all I had to do was casually swing my bat and it would go!'

'Amazing story José. I know you must have told it before but thank you again for sharing it with my readers and me.'

'Any time Mr Leman. I am always ready to share with my fans and all the supporters of the Kangaroo Giants.'

As José watches Mr Leman leave; he wonders if he should have shared more about himself, like his eye deformity. José had telescopic vision. What looked too many to be a baseball coming fast at you? It looked to José as an enormous beach ball slowly rotating towards him.

Oh, well, thought José, if I ever get bored in this career, I could become a private detective. I got an eye for details.

LOVE WAS JUST NOT READY FOR HER

How about you take me to dinner and a movie on Valentine's Day?'

'Oh Danielle, this is a splendidly wonderful idea for us to spend the evening together.'

'Anne, that is how Valentine's Day date was made. I had to initiate it. What do you think, Anne? Is Alex not sure about us?'

'OK Danielle, recap for me how you and Alex got together?'

'Alex and I have been going out for a solid six months and while we have some great times together, I sometimes feel that he is not ready to be in a relationship.'

'Now Anne. Alex is sweet and fun to be with, but he has given me some signs that he just might not be ready to have the same type of relationship I want.'

'Signs Danielle? What signs?'

'Oh, you know Anne. Women know them and can spot them. I went through a mental check to see which one is the most likely impediment to solidifying our relationship.'

'OK, Danielle, detail them for me.'

'First, it is possible that Alex was hurt in a previous relationship. Maybe Alex was dumped or rejected by someone he loved deeply. The pain is still too raw.'

'True Danielle. Has he ever spoken about anyone to you?'

'No, he has not. Let me continue with my thought process. I am going through all the signs he is emitting but might not be aware of. Like I said, second, it is possible he is focusing on his job and the pressures take a lot of his daily energies.'

'In the third spot, I think his friends take a lot of his time. At the pub, playing weekend semi-professional rugby leaves us with little time for us.'

'Oh Danielle, I did not know that. What else?'

'While we never spoke about it, we never really said to each other not to see other people. I have not gone out with anyone other than Alex all these months. What if he has? We are not exclusive. He can do what he wants, right? Is that a reason, I wonder?'

'By any chance, have you pressured him, Danielle? You know men push back when they are pressured.'

'No, I know I have not pressured him, at least consciously, but what if I have overstepped my boundaries and he thinks he is being pressured? I am confused with him and his feelings toward me, Anne.'

'Do you think he is seeing someone else? I worry about you, Danielle. I don't want you to feel you are in a Netflix drama series.'

'Goodness no Anne. I do not think he is seeing anyone else.'

'Well Danielle, then it has to be that you just have not 'turn on the right switch' for him to show you he is ready to commit to you.'

'What switch, Anne? What are you speaking about?'

'Listen sweetie, it has been my experience that men have certain innate switches like sex, food, drink, etc., that drive them. Maybe you just have not hit Alex's right switch yet?'

'Oh Anne, maybe I am not 'the one?'

'Danielle, tonight he will let you know if you are 'the one.'

'How Anne?'

'Is he picking you up?'

'Yes, at 7 PM tonight, for a nine o'clock movie, he said.'

'Well Danielle, if he is dressed nicer than normal, on time and has a reservation at a quaint restaurant and then he plans to take you to a romantic movie, say the remake of *West Side Story* by Steven Spielberg, then you know he is ready for you. If he does not do this, he will never commit. That has been my experience.'

'If these things do not happen. What do I do, Anne?'

'Follow your heart and call me in the morning. I got to run. Speak to you soon.'

As Anne left, Danielle looked at her watch and saw she had just an hour before Alex came to pick her up, so she got ready.

A quick shower, makeup and then the pièce de résistance, her new lace royal blue asymmetrical midi dress makes Danielle look stunning. She looks at her watch: 6:50 PM and she is ready with time to spare. Just relax; Alex will be here in a few minutes.

The doorbell rings and Danielle looks at her watch 7:40 PM. OK, so he is late but there is probably a good reason and she opens the door and sees Alex.

Alex has blue jeans, a red *'Big Bang Bazinga'* t-shirt and the ugliest runners she has ever seen. No socks.

'Hi, babe. Sorry I am late. Got caught up at the pub with the boys. I thought we head down to KFC, grab a box, and eat it on the way to watch the re-release of *Aliens*. Cool, yeah?'

Danielle just stood there for a few seconds when she thought that love was just not ready for her and slammed the door on Alex.

TOP 25 OF 68

Hey Jude, how are you today?'

'I am so-so Sally. Why is love blue?'

'Honey, Jude, why are you sitting here on the dock by the bay, anyway?'

Jude takes a long puff from his cigarette and gives Sally a funny answer. 'Just contemplating. You know. People got to be free to think.'

Not knowing for sure what that sentence meant, Sally changes course and asks: 'By the way, how is Gennie Robinson, the sunshine of your love?'

'Don't talk to me about her. I overheard a conversation between her and Judy.'

'Judy?'

'Yeah, the one in disguise, always wearing glasses.'

'Oh, that Judy. She is always looking weird. What did she say?'

'I overheard her tell Gennie; This guy is in love with you!'

'What guy Jude? You?'

'No. The way she described him was like he was someone else, for she specifically said three things about him.'

'What do you mean? What three things?'

'She said he was kind of the good, the bad and the ugly.'

'What in the world do you think Judy meant by that? I know that sometimes women will tell each other some midnight confessions.' Jude looked at Sally funny.

Sally had to clarify. 'It's the sort of thing women do, Jude; they share and when they do, they can cry like a baby. You know Gennie is a young girl. I went with my parents to the Harper Valley PTA monthly meeting and she seemed fine.'

'Sally, I am all confused. Last Friday night Gennie and I were dancing to the music when she stopped in the middle of a song, and said to me: hello, I love you, and then I thought of the crazy conversation I overheard. I do not know what to think. I wish it would rain so it can hide my hurt and my tears,' as Jude turns away from Sally.

'Now Jude, turn around, look at me and tighten up, boy. You know Gennie loves you. Remember the time both of you went to see her father in New York at his office in the Mony building?'

For a moment, Jude looked like he was in an old fashion stone soul picnic filled with alcohol and with a grin on his face he answered: 'Yeah, I thought it was a funny name for a company. It reminded me of that old song by Tommy James and the Shondells with a funny title, *'Mony, Mony.'*

'Jude, stop your mind from wandering off. Do you remember the story you told me about that trip or not?'

'Darn it Sally, of course, I do. We went to see Gennie's father in New York over at his estate in upper New York, but he was not there. He was working in the city and before we went into the city to see him, Gennie took me out to her paddock, where we got to go grazing in the grass for a while before we gave some little green apples to the horse. When we finished, we headed into the city to meet her father.'

'And what happened Jude when you met her father?'

'Nothing Sally, nothing happened,' as Jude gets up and trudges to the edge of the pier and all Sally hears is *la-la-la-la, means I love you*, as he jumps into the water.

THE SECOND TIME

O K Big Guy. You got it all in your head?'

'I think so, but should we go over all the fine points again before I start?'

Peter just bowed his head and wondered how many more times He needed to be shown. It is quite simple; really it is, or so thought Peter.

'OK, Big Guy, you got to have a plan. Why want to use social media? Are you trying to increase your online brand presence? Or are you trying to nurture relationships?'

'Yes, Peter, all of those things you mention.'

'You got to be confident when you start. You got to know how you are going to leverage your tweets. Understand?'

'Yes, I do. Go on.'

'Remember Big Guy; you must change the default Twitter avatar. Add your smiling face so people can see the real you. Then you must familiarise yourself with the settings. Be sure to enter your bio and uniform resource locator where people can further connect with you.'

'Got it. Anything else. It is all coming back to me from our first conversation. Go on, Peter.'

'Have you thought about the audience you are working to attract?'

'Come again, Peter. The audience?'

'Yes, big guy, the audience, the crowd. Who do you want to attract? What are their needs? What problems do they have? How can you help them solve problems?'

'Of course, yes, I know. My congregation. I have a good idea. Go on. This is so exciting. I cannot wait to get started.'

Peter lets off a very silent sign and continues.

'OK, you said you know it is your audience. You understand it is not about you, correct? The quicker you learn this, the better off you will be. Don't overcomplicate it. Your job is to remember to stop talking about yourself. Listen to your public, period!'

'Right, listen, don't talk. Got it. What else, Peter?'

'Do you have any idea where you are going to start?'

'Not really. Any suggestions?'

'There are three especially important points you must remember. Do you need to write them down?'

'No, I have excellent memory most of the time.'

'OK. First, start anywhere. There is no such thing as waiting for the perfect moment to start. There will never be a perfect time. On this platform, you must just jump in and go. Think of it as an imperfect perfection.'

'I don't work like that, Peter. You know I try to make perfect all the time.'

'I know, Big Guy, but that is the reality of the biz.'

After a few moments, Peter gets a nod to proceed.

'Don't be afraid to ask questions. Some humble soul will help you until you get your feet wet.'

'OK. I got it. Is that it?'

'No. It is critical that you listen as much, if not more, than you tweet. There may be days when you do not have to, but you must always be listening. Pay attention to the tone of conversations and the language your people are using, what topics they are sharing and talking about and how they connect with one another.'

'Wow. It is a lot to take in, that is for sure.'

'It is, but I know You can manage it. You do this by sharing value with your community and followers. And remember Big Guy, every tweet does not have to be a masterpiece. You are just starting out and while I know you are not a big talker, you must be precise with your tweets. You do not want to confuse anyone.'

'Yes, you are correct, Peter. No confused followers are necessary.'

'Also, as I mentioned earlier, do not make this about you. As often as possible, share other individuals' content. Find content that provides value to your target congregation and ideal follower. As you improve, you will self-teach this system and develop a winning strategy.'

'This is great stuff, Peter. That's it?'

'No. One more piece of advice.'

'What's that, Peter?'

'Be patient. You will not be a success overnight. Look how long it took your son. Over 2,000 years! So now we get to the end. Have any idea what your handle will be?'

'Oh yes, it is easy. I think I will be @god.'

'Big Guy, someone already took that handle. What are you going to do if you cannot use it?'

'Well, last time, I made it rain for forty days and forty nights and had them start over again. It should be just as easy the second time.'

CORRECTIONS

I was minding my business on the train yesterday when a tall man sat down next to me with a mysterious package. It was an unassuming little package, wrapped in brown paper and string, with no return address or any sign of who might have sent it. The man said nothing, just sat there looking at it for a long time.

By his attire, I guess he was a tailor. Don't ask me why I thought that he just looked like a tailor. His suit style was odd and seemed almost Victorian, but I am not the fashion police, so I did not care how he dressed. As time passed, I was getting a little uncomfortable, wondering what was inside the package and why the man was just sitting there staring at it.

Eventually, I couldn't take it anymore and I asked him what was inside. He just smiled and said, 'You'll see,' before getting up, leaving the package on the seat next to me and getting off at the next stop.

Now what? The man left the package behind and tempted me to open it myself. Looking at the package itself did not help me discern what was in it, but it was definitely suspicious. I'm glad that I didn't open it! I'm still shaken up about it. I decided if the conductor came by, I would ask him to remove it.

The only thing I could think of was: 'OK, Big Guy. You got crazy thoughts in your head!'

The package just rested there on the seat next to me.

A short man rushed into the carriage at the next station, all excited. I wondered why the man was so excited as he rushed into the carriage and then he just sat down across from me. When he sat down, he didn't say a word to me at all until he saw the package.

Finally, he spoke up. 'Hey, what's in the box?'

Shrugging my shoulders, I was getting ready to answer him. I did not know when he said: 'Was that left here by a tall man?'

Startled at his question, I dumbly nodded my head.

He just smiled, reached over, and grabbed the package as we reached the next stop.

'What are you going to do?' I asked.

'You'll see,' as he rushes to the exit.

I couldn't wait to see what it could be, so I hopped off the train and followed him. We walked down a long alley when he stopped in front of a door and knocked.

An old woman answered the door and invited us in. 'Siediti e ti porterò qualcosa da bere,' she said.

It sounded Italian, and I did not speak the language but her body mannerism told me to take a stool by the table while the man from the train stood holding the package. The old woman came in with two beer mugs, each with a wonderful-looking head on it steadily held in one hand and a long, rectangular box in the other. She handed it to me and said: 'Aprilo' and mimics a child opening a present. I nodded. I understood and opened it.

Inside was a black cloth, about a foot and a half wide, and a foot and a half long. I stared in wonder at the strange object. It looked like nothing I had ever seen and the only way I could describe it was it looked like a pipe. 'Prendi questo,' she said. 'Ne haibi sogno.'

Again, the man from the train just stood there holding his own box and smiling.

I took the old pipe and scrutinised it. It was a well-preserved cherry-wood pipe similar to the ones mentioned in Arthur Conan Doyle stories about his famous detective Holmes. After a minute of inspecting the pipe, I return the pipe to the woman who places it on the table.

'Ieri abbiamo fatto una gita fuori città al mare,' said the old woman.

'What did you say?' I asked.

'Ieri abbiamo fatto una gita al mare,' answered the woman again, and she left us alone to talk.

Noticing I had a confused face on me, the man translates for me.

'She said: We went on a trip to the sea yesterday.'

Now I was confused. An Italian woman is telling me she went to the sea yesterday with someone and is now showing me a cherry-wood pipe. What is going on? I thought to myself.

Sensing confusion, the man explains.

'Professor Brown, I would have thought you would have recognised the pipe. Do you not know to whom the pipe belongs?'

'How do you know my name? Who are you? What is going on? I demand answers right now!'

'Obviously, you do not recognise me. Please inspect.'

I stepped back and gave the man a better look. He is an average-sized built with a square jaw, a thick neck, and a moustache. Now that I looked at him better, he also dressed in a Victorian style business suit. Strange that I had not noticed this when he rushed into the train.

'Sorry, I do not recognise you. Have you attended any of my lectures? That could be the only reason you know me. Am I correct?'

With a big smile, he answers. 'No Professor Brown. You have author over two-hundred articles and books about my colleague and me. Most of it is correct except for one point.'

My face must have been blank for he then opened the box he held and came up a calabash.

'Why, that is my valuable calabash! I have it on display on my mantle over my fireplace at home. It is priceless. What is this? You stole this from my home, did you not?'

'Well, yes and no. My colleague did and left it for me on the train when he sat next to you in order for me to give to you now. He also entrusted me to share with you the truth. My colleague never used a calabash. He enjoyed tobacco in a blackened clay pipe, an oily briar, and a cherry wood. That cherry wood you now hold in your hand, Professor.'

Suddenly, it sank in. It could not be. It is now the year 2023, and it just made little sense. The character that used the pipes would have used them between the years of 1880 and 1914. He could not be alive and, more to the point, he is a fictional character!

'No. That is impossible. You are telling me you are his trusted partner?'

'Yes, I am. At your service.'

I had placed the beer on the table and now I picked it up and gulped it down.

'No. I do not believe you are who you said you are because that would mean that the individual who sat next to me on the train is……...'

'Yes, he is Professor. We would like for you to take a moment and contact your publishers and amend all the articles and books where you mention he used the calabash and insert one of the other three pipes.'

Looking at him, I realise that he too is a fictional character and over one hundred years old and yet here I am sitting with him and discussing the various pipes used by his sleuthing partner.

'OK, I will do as you ask, but I need to set up a time to interview both of you. This is absolutely amazing and it will set off a firestorm in the literary world.'

'That is not possible, Professor. Neither he nor I will adhere to that request, for we are far too busy solving cases. Please just make the corrections as soon as possible. These corrections will be just elementary.'

Dr Watson takes the cherry-wood pipe from the table and leaves me sitting there with the calabash to figure out how to correct all my articles and books.

Elementary indeed.

IDIOT

Now tell me exactly what do you think was stolen this time, Mr Diamond?'

Bill Diamond, the owner of Diamond's Jewellery in Northport New South Wales, looks at Detective Inspector Jessica Maguire and is just mesmerise by her angelic face.

Six weeks ago, there was a break in his store and just a few items were stolen; he only itemised about $50,000 worth of items which was just under his excess with the insurance company which meant no insurance payout but still if he could recover the jewellery he would not be out of pocket. That was all of Bill's concern until the detective walked into his store.

A devout bachelor who enjoys the company of ladies, Bill never had a relationship that lasted over six months. It was always his choice to breakup with lame excuses.

'It's not you; it's me,'

'My work is too demanding to have a meaningful relationship,'

'You're too good for me.'

'I need some space.'

'You will outgrow me, and I could not stand that pain.'

'Our zodiac signs are not compatible.'

'We love each other too much.'

Bill always thought that if these excuses worked, without regard for the other feelings, then why should he worry about it? Besides, he had many more to use if necessary.

But then in came Detective Jessica Maguire.

Six weeks ago, she walked in looking marvellously. She wore a dark blue tailored pantsuit cut low on the waist where her gun clip lived and a white blouse displaying just her right neck while holding a fine chain necklace with a tiny trinket. She wore her hair short, used a little makeup, and had manicured nails. Simple and stunning at the same time. Bill could not get enough of her. Today, she looked just as stunning.

'Mr Diamond, can you tell me what they took this time?'

Bill glances quickly at the constable that is firmly standing by his front door and hands the detective a list and she glimpses at it.

'It looks very similar to the previous four times. You said that the CCTV was not working again?'

'Correct Detective Maguire. They must have figured a way to bypass the security, so I have no film.'

A slight frown appears on the detective's face while she looks at the constable, but it quickly goes away.

'Mr Diamond, I find it very peculiar that out of all the jewellery stores in Northport, yours is the only one being targeted all the time. Is there someone who has a grudge against you? Someone who is just harassing you. Any ideas?'

'No Detective Maguire, may I call you Jessica, by the way?'

'I prefer Detective or Detective Maguire, Mr Diamond.'

Taken aback by the abrupt response, Bill continues answering the question.

'Oh, OK. I have had no run-ins with anyone or a disgruntle customer. I am the sole employee, so if someone has beef with me, they have to be an outside source. Am I saying all the right words in describing my circumstance? I want to be as much help as possible but of course, you can always come back and visit and ask me more questions. Any time.'

Bill was just ecstatic that the detective might just do that but received quite a surprise.

'No Mr Diamond. I have no more questions and I do not think I will return soon. I think I know what is happening here. Could you please come from behind the counter and stand in front of me?'

Great, thought Bill. I made an impression, and she now wants a closer, maybe even more intimate, moment. She might just reach around my neck and place a big, slow, sweet kiss on my lips.

As Bill comes behind the counter and stops in front of the detective, she extends her hand, which Bill gladly reaches for when she suddenly grabs it, spins him around, and puts handcuffs on him.

'Bill Diamond, I am arresting you for giving false and misleading information to the police under section 307B of the Crimes Act 1900 in New South Wales, which carries a maximum penalty of 2 years in prison. You are not obliged to say or do anything unless you wish to do so, but whatever you say or do may be used in evidence. Do you understand?'

Bill is stunned. What happens? How did she figure out he was tripping the alarm on purpose in order for her to come and visit him?

'Detective. Jessica. I thought you knew I am in love with you. Don't you care about me? What reason do you have not to want to be with me? Please do not give me a lame excuse.'

'A lame excuse, Mr Diamond? How about this excuse I have a career to think of?'

As the Detective hands Bill to the constable to the waiting car, she goes behind the counter and finds the key to lock the front door. Locking it, Jessica looks at Bill as the constable sits Bill in the car and thinks to herself.

'Idiot.'

MYSTERY WRITER

G osh, I hate Mondays,' thought aspiring mystery writer Joaquin Navarro as he comes out of his unit above the town's only optician store and walks by its bookstore, Village Books & Stuff. Joaquin looks through the window at the books on display and an attractive cover catches his eye: *Stories to Share with My Partner-Book 1*. He mumbles to himself: 'I might just come in on Thursday after work and pick it up. It looks like a fun book, just by its cover.'

Looking at his watch, Joaquin notices he is cutting close to catching the 7:50 **AM**, so he picks up his pace. Picking up his pace was not an issue for Joaquin.

He is a junior market analyst for one of the big accounting firms that specialise in venture capital and while he sits in front of a computer for most of the day, he tries to make up for this laxity while at work with a rigorous forty-five-minute workout in the company's gym, followed by a quick shower and a light lunch. After clocking out at 6 PM sharp, Joaquin returns to the gym for a short thirty-minute workout, again a quick shower catching the 7:20 PM home, which gets him to his front door at 8:20 PM sharp. Like clockwork.

This precision allows Joaquin to devote several hours after dinner to his mystery writing, which he envisions one day to be displayed in the bookstore below.

But Mondays are always hard.

The weekend, especially Saturday, is his 'R & R' day in which he meets his friends and sometimes catches up with other local writers to discuss plots, strategies, etc. This leaves him with Sunday to rest, bum around in his unit and just plain get away from his daily life and dream of his current novel and how it is going.

Every day, nothing happens. Joaquin wears his earbuds on the way to work, listening to his favourite authors. Cussler, Patterson, Nodar, you know the great ones, and being the middle of winter in Sydney, his overcoat on his daily train trek; he's ignored, and he ignores.

Then one evening, on his way home from another stressful day at the office, Joaquin is startled out of his funk when a frantic Asian man knocks him over at a dead run, then races up the stairs—pursued by two thugs. Joaquin sees the thug raise a revolver, and a shot rings through the cavernous Central station.

They shot the Asian man.

From his position on the floor, Joaquin watches hundreds of people scatter and crouch behind columns, expecting more shots that do not come. One shot was all it took to bring the Asian man down. The thugs kneel by the Asian man and start searching him but stop when they hear someone shouting 'Police. Police. They are over there,' and they quickly escape through one of the many exits and just disappear into the street.

Joaquin gets up and starts dusting himself as he watches the police stand next to the body and create a makeshift cordon around it as more officers arrive. As he dusts his overcoat, he discovers a small package in the side pocket.

Taking the package out, he slowly opens it and finds a fluffy fake rabbit fur key chain with one key attached and an encrypted note with some words typed in lowercase: 4528 Lewis Street, Spring Farm NSW-igygyb!

Surprised at the key chain and the strange note, Joaquin did not notice the police had moved the body. Looking at the spot where the Asian man fell, there was no blood, and he wondered how the police or the train custodians had cleaned up the mess so quickly. Shrugging his shoulders, he goes to the platform just in time for his 7:20 PM train.

Hopping into the carriage and quickly finding a seat by the window, he holds the note in his left hand and reads it again.

It just made little sense.

The key chain was a puzzle because he wondered what the key was. It looked like any key you might have in the office or in a home. But the note, the strange note with the address and then the letters 'igygyb,' that is strange. A mystery indeed, but then Joaquin says to himself: 'hey, you are a mystery writer; you should be able to figures this out.'

Arriving at his unit at exactly 8:20 PM, he quickly changes, grabs his car keys, and walks down the back door to the car park. Sitting in the car and before starting the car, Joaquin keys the address into the built in GPS screen of his Mini John Cooper Works Clubman. 'Only thirty-two minutes.' Reversing and quickly accessing the main drag of Northport, he heads toward the southern road and after what seemed less than thirty-two minutes, Joaquin arrives at 4528 Lewis Street Spring Farm.

A beautiful Hampton style with a wrap-around porch presents the single-storey building. Joaquin walks up to the front door and rings the doorbell and waits.

Nothing.

No one comes to the door.

He turns to leave and thinks twice about it. He has a key on a fuzzy fake rabbit key chain. Will the key fit this door?

Inserting the key into the lock, he hears the tumbler turn and the door gingerly opens to his hand.

'Hello. Anyone home?'

Walking in further down the long hall, he sees a lot of closed doors but decides not to venture into any of them and continues to what appears to be the lounge where sitting propped up on the three-seater lounge is the Asian man looking lifeless.

'Oh crap!' thinks Joaquin to himself. 'What did I get myself into? My fingerprints are on the door handle. I rang the doorbell. The police are going…'

'Wait, a minute,' stopping his thought in mid-air. 'How did the Asian man's body get here? The police would not bring him here. They would take him to the hospital, the morgue, or somewhere else, but not to his home. Is this his home?' Joaquin is stumped and moves in closer to have a better look at the body.

Gradually he moves toward the lounge and when he gets within a metre of the body, the Asian man jumps up!

A startled Joaquin almost faints and quickly turns and starts running and he bumps into Harry McDonald, his hot desk colleague at work who is laughing energetically.

'Totally worth it. The look on your face, Joaquin. I will never forget it as long as I live. The experience was amazing!'

'What the…? What is going on, Harry? What are you doing here? Who is this man? Whose house is this?'

'Relax Joaquin. It is pay-back time, that all.'

'Pay-back time? For what, Harry?'

'For all those children's pranks you pulled on me in the office. The Whoopi cushion, the dribble cup, the fake dog poop on my chair, the stupid fake snake in the can joke, those fake bug ice cubes at the Christmas party. Need I go on?'

'Damn it, Harry, I could have given me a heart attack.'

'In your excellent shape? That would not happen.'

'Well, I got to go. So, I bid you adieu.'

'Wait Harry. What in the world is igygyb?'

'Why I thought you would figure it out, you mystery writer. It means I Got You Good You Bastard.'

MARRIAGE

To some, it's a blissful union,

To others, it's a nightmare.

Some say that marriage is love,

Some say it's just a bond.

Others say that marriage is a
puzzle,

That you have all the pieces and all
you need is the key

If that is the case

You are the key and I found the key
to love.

And it's YOU,

YOU,

YOU,

YOU.

CHINESE STIR-FRIED CHICKEN

Jericho is one of the oldest European settlements in western New South Wales. The community is of great significance to the Wilyakali people who traditionally occupied the lands around Broken Hill. Jericho is about 1,100 kilometres from Sydney using the B94 and about sixty kilometres from Broken Hill.

The hamlet of Jericho is a lot smaller than the town of Broken Hill. Jericho has just a little over one-thousand inhabitants compared to the seventeen plus population in Broken Hill. Australians know Broken Hill for its mining history and the geology exhibits at the Albert Kersten Mining and Minerals Museum. Jericho, well, it has a police substation.

Senior Sergeant Arely Socket transferred from Broken Hill to a supposed promotion in Jericho, but Arely was not too sure it was a promotion. He always wondered why Jericho needed to have a police sub-station but did not bother to research it or even ask about it during his interview.

Arely arrived in Jericho to find he had a staff of three constables and one office manager to patrol the town, which covers an area of approximately 195 square kilometres comprising Jericho and the smaller hamlet of Menindee. At first, Arely was worried that his workforce could not cope with a crime in such a large area but in the last year since his posting, he has only dealt with a few pub incidents, some missing petrol cans, and a few treed cats in this God-forsaken part of the state.

When he got a call at police headquarters from Yindi Carmichael, his only female constable, it made for an interesting morning.

'Chief, you got to come to the cemetery, quick?'

Arely enjoyed being called chief and while he had a long way to go from Senior Sergeant to Chief Inspector, it had a nice ring to it.

'What's up, Yindi? Why are you at the cemetery?'

'Normal patrol Chief. You got to come down and see it. I don't want to speak over the mobile.'

'Right. OK, see you in twenty.'

Looking at his watch, Arely noticed it was only 7:50 AM. The sun had barely come up an hour ago and Yindi already had found an incident to report. Probably graffiti, but she asked and a good chief supports his officers. Again, Arely loved the sound of that word: chief.

Arriving at the cemetery a bit after 8 AM, he spots Yindi standing close to a tombstone. As he approaches Yindi, he sees a freshly dug grave and notices Yindi pointing at it. Arely looks in the grave and sees a headless nude male corpse.

'Damn,' he says aloud.

'Yes Chief. That is the same thing I said when I walked up to it. I checked and besides the blank tombstone, there is no sign of who he is.'

Arely walks around the dug up grave and cannot see any unusual activity. Checking his watch, Arely knew that Katherine Paterson, Broken Hill's coroner, would be in the office and he could call her to help.

'Yindi, I hate to make you stay, but I am calling Dr Paterson to get the body and see if she can run some tests to see how the man was killed and find out who he is by checking his fingerprints. Wait until she arrives, then mark off the area once they leave with the body.'

'Right chief. I got it.'

Arely sits in his patrol car, dials the morgue, and gets a quick answer: 'Morgue. Dr Paterson speaking.'

'Hi, Katherine. Arely here. Got a body and need answers quick.'

'A good morning to you as well, Arely. Where is the deceased?'

'In the cemetery.'

Arely heard a quick giggle before there was an answer: 'Isn't that the logical place for a body, Arely? You're not pulling a prank on me this early, are you? I just barely finished my first-morning coffee.'

'No Katherine. It's for real. Yindi is standing watch until you and your team get here. How long before you can come?'

'About forty-five minutes.'

'Good. I'll let Yindi know. Let me know when you have some answers.'

'Oui Monsieur. Feramon capitaine.'

'Quit showing off your recent trip to France. I need answers quick,' as he hangs up.

Arely knew Katherine when he was in Broken Hill. While a coroner is a special magistrate associated with local courts and is legally trained, the coroner doesn't need to have a medical qualification but Kathrine is an MD which gives heavier credence to her testimony.

As Arely drives back to Jericho, his mind works on his plan to tackle his first murder in Jericho in God knows how many years. He will have to check the archives to see if anything is there that might help.

At noon Marnie, the office manager, calls out: 'Chief, Mrs Quigley, on line two.'

'Now what?' Arely thinks as he picks up the line.

'Senior Sergeant Socket. How can I help you, Mrs Quigley?'

'Ah Sergeant Socket, so glad you are in. Munchie is the tree again.'

This was the fourth time in three months. Arely hated Munchie.

'Mrs Quigley, how long has the cat been on the tree?'

'About ten minutes, Sergeant.'

'Then give the cat some time up there and it will come down on its own.'

'But Sergeant, it's lunch time, and she has not come down.'

Looking at the wall clock, Arely sees the time: 10:30 AM.

'Mrs Quigley, it is 10:30 AM. I am sure it is not the cat's lunch time yet. Wait until at least noon.'

'Sergeant Socket, I will have you know that my lunch is between 10:30 AM and 11 AM every day and it has been so for the past fifteen years, so don't tell me what time it is to have my lunch.'

'Sorry Mrs Quigley, please have your lunch and I will have one of my officers come by to help as soon as possible.'

'But Munchie responds to your voice so much better. She finds it soothing and comes down when you call her to do so.'

Hmm, thought Arely; he remembers yelling at the damn cat, not talking it down. Oh, well, he can always get a quick bite afterwards in town.

'OK Mrs Quigley, I will be around noon. Call back if the cat comes down before 11:30 AM, so I avoid the trip, OK?'

'Munchie.'

'What Mrs Quigley?'

'Munchie is her name. Show some respect Sergeant,' and she hangs up.

'Great. Another happy citizen,' as Arely dials for Marnie.

'Yes Chief.'

'How far back do the archives go? Do you recall the last time the force used them?'

'Crickey, Chief, I do not know and I do not remember anyone ever going there in the last twenty, twenty-five years since I been here.'

'Alright, find me the key and I will go look myself.'

Ten minutes later, Marnie hands Arely the keys and he walks to the back of the station to the records area. He unlocks the door, and he seems to walk into the past.

Dust, even a few cobwebs, are on some of the shelving. No one ever seems to come in here, not since every case started getting digitised in December 2020. Arely was sure that no one ever thought of calling Jericho's station for their old records to be digitised.

Today, criminologists group crimes into five major categories: violent crime; property crime; white-collar crime; organized crime; and consensual or victimless crime. Arely loved the thought process brought into the records department in Jericho in its earlier days. They also catalogued cases as to the crime, but they fell into three categories: theft, vagrancy, and others.

This was going to be easy research thought Arely and proving his up-and-coming skills as a detective, he picked up the first few boxes starting with the one labelled: 'Others-1853-1899' and 'Others-1900-1930' Two boxes and three boxes to go.

Why he started with the earlier boxes, he did not know. Maybe curiosity as to the past of Jericho's criminal activities that fell into the 'others' category. Maybe he needed to spend time in his office. Arely was unsure, but he picked them up and returned them to his office.

He first sees a checklist accounting for the cases with a simple paragraph detailing the crime. This was even going to be easier, but it was a reasonably large box, so it took him about an hour on the first box before Mrs Quigley calling to say the darn cat had come down and he need not come. Then Yindi reported that Katherine had just left with the body.

The phone had not rung since then. Good, he had plenty of time to read.

Looking at the wall clock, he sees that is after 1 PM and asks Marnie to bring him a coffee and a sandwich from Franco's deli down the street and to get herself a coffee and hands her a couple of notes.

As Marnie leaves to get his lunch, Arely smiles. He has been in Franco's place before and was an ex-Afghan army colonel that left the country when it fell to the Taliban ran it. How he ended up in Jericho Arely did not ask. Maybe he was also promoted, he thought, smiling once more.

Using the checklist made the research even easier and having completed the first box, the answer was simple-no violent crimes of any kind, so he starts on box number two when Marnie walks in with his lunch and change and nods her thanks for her coffee.

The coffee smelled good, and the sandwich was decent enough as he continues with his research of box two when the checklist almost screams out at him: nothing.

'Great' Arely thinks. Unless there is a murder case in the next three boxes, I will oversee my first murder cases myself unless headquarters sends in a detective.

'Chief, Dr Paterson is on line two.'

'Katherine, if you are calling with results, that is quick. What you got?'

'Hello Arely, I'm fine, by the way. Yes, I am calling you with some information but I have not received all the information but from preliminary observation I know who the individual is.'

'So, what do the fingerprints say he is?'

'No, I have not received the fingerprint information yet; still waiting.'

'How can you tell who he is, then?'

There is a slight pause before Katherine answers. 'He has a birthmark on the inside of his left leg, next to his groin. That is how I think I know who he is.'

Now is Arely's turn to remain quiet for a moment or two.

'Please explain.'

'Well Arely, I just ended a relationship with a man during my trip to France when I found out then he was married. He has the identical birthmark, so I am guessing it is him.'

'I need the name and address of the individual you had the relationship with Katherine.'

Arely takes down the information and does a quick internet search.

'Katherine, don't leave the morgue until you get the fingerprint results. I will swing by soon. OK?'

'Of course, Arely. I will wait for the results until you come.'

Arriving at the address, he notices a Lexus RX with its rear hatch open and a couple of suitcases ready to load in the driveway. As he approaches the front door, a heavy-set woman with another suitcase sees him and the patrol car. She tosses the suitcase in Arely's face and runs toward the back of the house.

Catching the suitcase and pushing it to the ground, Arely gives chase, but it was not much of a chase. She had a dress and high heels and was not fast at all, so she was easy to catch with a simple use of his baton whacking her leg. She loses her balance and falls flat in the luscious green grass.

'I'm sorry, I'm sorry. I did not mean to do it. we had a simple fight. I caught him on a lie. He said he had gone to France on a business trip and turned out he was with some floosy and was going to break off our marriage for her. I got mad and struck him with my cast iron wok when I was making Chinese stir-fried chicken last night. I'm so sorry.'

Handcuffing her, Arely recites his memorised statement. 'You have the right to remain silent. You have the right to an attorney; if you cannot afford one, one will be appointed for you. If you waive these rights and talk to us, anything you say may be used against you in court.' By the way, what is your name?

'Marlene Thompson.'

'Let go to the station Marlene, where you can repeat what you said to me and I recorded on my body cam.'

With a sad face, Marlene gets into the patrol car and as Arely drives back to the station, he thinks to himself: 'Whatever would have possessed her to cut his head off? Why would she want to bury him naked? Was she able to carry him by herself into the car and then dig the hole to throw him in it?'

Looking through the rear-view mirror, Arely thought: 'Yes, she could definitely do these things. What possessed her? Simple. Rage. Bury him naked? Degradation. Carry him into the car and toss him to the ground? Easy. She definitely is hefty enough. I am sure I will get her version at the station.'

Looking at the road ahead, Arely had one more thought: 'What will I have for dinner tonight? Chinese stir-fried sounds good.'

COORDINATES

Chisis looked at his instruments like he has done so many times since the start of this trip. As the ship's navigator, he has taken every possibility to make sure everything is running perfectly. From the simplest to the more complex. Simple things like speed, heading and many more other crucial information in intergalactic flight. All indicators showed Chisis was doing the right thing, just as he was trained. His speed indicator shows the speed at precisely three per secs as instructed by his commander. Chisis also maintained the ship's artificial gravity generator at what the Commander referred to as the 'sweet spot', making it possible for the crew to be comfortable at all times.

Everything was great, as always, so it bore Chisis out of his mind.

He glances at the communications officer Akila and sees her fiddling with the instruments. Always alert, ever so conscious of her responsibility. That tenacity is why he cannot keep his mind off her. Add to that her intelligence and she is not bad looking either, so quite a combo thought Chisis, yet he could never ask her to a meal at the mess hall.

'Stupid Chisis,' his older brother Asim would say.

'Ensign Chisis, are you daydreaming again?' says Commander Amenhotep as he walks onto the command deck.

'No, Commander Amenhotep, just calculating how much longer we have to arrive at the next coordinates.'

'It is my calculation, and science officer Sadig concurs. We have about one hour. Let me turn on the visuals for you, sir.'

A view screen pops up, and a magnified sphere of a planet appears, looking beautifully like a blue circular form with white swirls. You can see brown, yellow, green, and white parts. Quite a scene thought Chisis.

'And the distress signals are coming from which coordinates, Ensign?'

'We have three different signals, Commander. The first one is from 29.9723° N, 31.1285° E, followed by 29.9759° N, 31.1309° E and then the final one at 29.9792° N, 31.1342° E.,' answers Chisis.

'You received three distress signals? That makes little sense. Your opinion Ensign Akila?'

'Commander Amenhotep, I do not believe these are distress signals but directional signals.'

'Explain Ensign.'

'Sir, when the Kawkab left our world, it was staffed by an experienced crew looking for new worlds for our growing population to populate. It is possible that they found this planet not to be suitable and left us these directional coordinates for us. I believe they intend for us to bypass the planet, Sir because of how the individual coordinates are given.'

'Seems logical,' thought the Commander, but he asked another question.

'Then explain Ensign Akila, why three coordinates?'

Standing up, Akila looks at the commander and answers: 'I believe Commander Amenhotep that the Kawkab commander is telling us to turn. That this is not the planet we are looking for our mass migration,' as Akila takes her hand and points int in a curved fashion to the right. 'They mean for us to turn right, Sir.'

Commander Amenhotep thought of the Kawkab commander, Commander Omari. He bunked with him at the academy and always liked him. Omari was a cautious student but was not afraid to investigate, and if the ensign is correct, then the three directional coordinates are more of a warning as well, for the inhabitants of the planet might not welcome them. Commander Amenhotep also knew the ship's counsellor Dalila from the academy. A bright woman who was gentle in her counsel but firm with her convictions and she would have supported Omari in his judgement.

His ship the Almajara is the most advance in the homeland's fleet and can manage any situation, but Commander Amenhotep is also a cautious commander or he would not have survived this long in the fleet.

'Chisis, can you get me a visual on all the three coordinates at the same time?'

'Yes commander, that is possible. One moment.'

As the commander waited for the visuals to come online, he contacted his security captain, Bahiti, who responds in seconds.

'Yes Commander. How can I help?'

Commander Amenhotep thought that a female Bahiti was physically strong enough to take down a much larger male, but had the softest of voices for such a fierce soldier.

'Bahiti, if we were to land on this planet, are your troopers ready for anything that might endanger the Almajara?'

'Yes Commander Amenhotep. To the end.'

'I do not think it will come to that Bahiti, but I need you to prepare for the worst scenario possible.'

'Yes Commander Amenhotep,' and the communication cuts off as Chisis alerts the Commander that the visuals are ready to view.

'Put them on view,' a little perturbed Amenhotep replies.

The visuals come online and show three structures aligning with the coordinates received from the signals. All three structures are similar but offer varied sizes. The smallest structure is at 29.9759° N, 31.1309° E coordinates has each side of its measures one-hundred-nine metres, while its height is sixty-six metres.

The second structure is a little larger, measuring two-hundred-sixteen metres on each side and one-hundred-forty-three metres high.

The largest structure from where the signals are emitting has a length of each side at the base averaging two-hundred-thirty metres and I estimated its height at one-hundred-forty-seven metres.

'Chisis, can you magnify those little dots around the structures?'

'No Commander Amenhotep. We are at maximum magnification.'

'I am going to my ready room. Hold our position and do not advance closer to the planet, understood Chisis?'

'Yes Commander.'

Commander Amenhotep sits at his desk and, for once, he feels the weight of command for the first time. He has experienced battles and emergencies which he transitioned through with some scars but was successful. This time a wrong decision not only may doom the Almajara but his entire species. Is this a sign from Omari? Is Ensign Akila correct? The structures do seem to form an arc pointing to the right. There is only one way to be certain, thinks the commander as he reaches for his communicator and he calls Bahiti. 'Are you ready?'

'Yes Commander, on your command.'

'What is your status?'

'Commander, I have a platoon of troopers ready to go at your command, Sir.'

'No. Thirty-six troopers are too much. It might stir something that may not be necessary. Include yourself in a reconnaissance team taking only the troopers and try to find out what those moving dots are. Do not engage. Just observe, document, and report back as soon as possible. Questions Bahiti?'

'Sir, if we encounter danger, do we engage?'

'Negative. Avoid any confrontation. You are there for a recon mission and report back to me in person. Understood?'

'Yes Commander.'

After six minutes, Commander Amenhotep receives a communication message that the Zahal had departed the docking station and was heading for the planet. All Amenhotep could do was wait and hope that Bahiti would not have to engage whatever or whoever was next to the structures.

The hours pass and it is not only Commander Amenhotep that is sitting at their stations waiting to hear what Bahiti and her troopers have found out about the mysterious dots around the structures.

Looking at her instruments, Akila notices an incoming message from the recon mission and quickly passes the information to her commander.

Ten minutes later, Bahiti is standing in front of her commander, who is anxiously waiting for her report.

'Sir, as you instructed us, we landed near the structures and using our cloaking system, we remained quite hidden and we stated our observations as instructed.'

Commander Amenhotep nods for her to continue.

'Immediately after landing we determine the dots are inhabitants of the planet are part of a lesser form of species that like to stand around the structure and use a primitive type of artifact to point at the structures as if trying to read for signs. Some stand in front of the structures, while one of the species uses the same artifact to point to them. For some reason,

I could not determine whether the inhabitants take their appendages, point to the structures, and make strange movements with their apparent faces. Quite strange Sir.'

'Do they seem hostile?'

'Sir, we were ready for action but the answer is no. they do not seem hostile, Sir. We noticed that sometimes, after finishing pointing their artifacts at each other, they raise their appendages, slap them high over their heads, and seem pleased about it. Again, Sir, very odd customs or mannerisms. I am not sure how to categorise them.'

'We intercepted one of their artifact conversations, Sir. With the help of Akila using the universal translation communicator, we believe we can successfully hear what they said in our language. It is a conversation between two females of the species. Would you like to hear it?'

'Yes, I do. It might help me determine the next course of action.'

Bahiti hits her communication button and plays the bizarre conversation with the commander.

Voice One: 'Hey, let's play a game,'

Voice Two: 'Um, OK,'

Voice One: 'I bet I can get you to say red, ready?'

Voice Two: 'Yeah.'

Voice One: 'What colour is the sky?'

Voice Two: 'Blue'

Voice One: 'Told you I could get you to say blue.'

Voice Two: 'Wait, no you said red.'

Voice One: 'Boom! You said red.'

Voice Two: 'Dang!'

'The conversation ceased after that Commander and we could not capture it again, but we had many similar and even worse interceptions between many of the inhabitants around the structures.'

Commander Amenhotep takes a few minutes and makes what will be his best commanding decision.

'Chisis, if you follow the directions, what course will it take us?'

'Sir, we would turn right on the planet.'

'Do it.'

'Yes, Sir.'

'Thank your trooper for their courage to venture down to the planet for me, Bahiti. I will certainly update your profile to note extreme confidence while doing your duties.'

'Thank you, commander. Since we are departing, may I show you a hologram of a strange poster we saw as you get closer to the structures?'

'Of course, Bahiti.'

Bahiti places her communication button on the commander's desk and presses a button and a projection appears and it shows a poster with the following symbols on it: 'WELCOME TO THE GREAT PYRAMIDS OF GIZA.'

'Thank you Bahiti, for showing me those strange symbols. I believe I made the right decision for the Almajara and our species. This planet seems to be filled with weird inhabitants.'

'You absolutely did, Sir,' as Bahiti leaves the commander's ready room to return to her station.

MEAL SELECTION

As darkness fell and the waves became a gentle rolling sound, he tried not to sleep. Pablo had heard the stories pass down for generations by his family. His great grandfather was one, then his grandfather, then his father, and now he is one. A pishtaco.

As Pablo laid on his hammock on his ocean front beach house in Mancora, Peru, his thoughts drifted to his family's history.

Known to roam the Andes and suck the fat from peasants, they describe the pishtaco as a pale-skinned vampire by the few that survived to tell about him. Many have described this immortal as a male who masquerades itself as a doctor, peasant, traveller, and even a priest.

Pablo knew that this terrifying creature wasn't a figment of imagination but a legend of true events.

The Cordillera de Los Andes forms a continuous highland along the western edge of South America. This is where his family had lived for generations until the Spaniards arrived, which for Pablo's family was also a blessing in disguise. The Spanish power and influence extended from the north to south through seven South American countries: Venezuela, Colombia, Ecuador, Peru, Bolivia, Chile, and Argentina. This presented an opportunity for Pablo's family.

The new invaders are blamed for any deeds by the pishtacos and so the legends continued over the centuries and the blame piled up on the Spaniards as they maintained their stronghold on the vast land.

But things changed as the populace revolted to Spanish rule and Pablo's family had to adapt to the changing world.

Adapt they did. They did very well.

Hunger is a formidable drive for Pablo and his family. Over the centuries, the inhabitants adapted to the new Spaniard cuisine, and the population grew to Pablo's family delight. The population grew not only in numbers but in girth as they introduced more starch to the daily diet. As the populace grew in numbers, Pablo's family feasted more, but they were now also more noticeable.

The Spaniards became suspicious, so Pablo's family had to become cautious, but still, they feasted. When the Spaniards were expelled, the local 'Guardia' transferred their responsibilities to the national police force, the PNP, and the family had to devise a new strategy.

Pablo's family had become affluent over the centuries and well educated, and this had given Pablo an idea. At first, the family's scepticism sprung from them, but when he put his own money into the venture, and as success grew, his elders started pouring funds into it as well.

Pablo's brilliant idea was so simple that only a pishtaco could have thought of it, he thought. Instead of worrying that the local population would go on the worldwide fad of 'eating healthy,' Pablo invested all his money in the first local McDonald's in the Mancora beach town and before you knew it, the 'ArcosDorados' had blossomed to over thirty in the local province.

Laughter interrupted his thoughts coming down from the beach. He looks and sees a small group of teenagers sitting around an open fire eating, and he smiles as he sees large bags of hamburgers from his local store.

Pablo thought, " oh well, " I best get some dinner myself as he heads toward the shore for his selection.

TELE-NOVELLA

The noise is unbearable. Long-haul trucks, soup-up hot rods, old gas guzzlers from a bygone era whizzing by at high speeds, day and night and the police doing nothing or not caring about it, thought Francisco Miguel, Frankie to his roommates and friends, as he laid on his single bed looking up at the freshly painted ceiling.

Ah America.

The land of opportunity.

Streets paved in gold or so thought his parents when they left Cuba during the Cuban missile crisis in 1962 and settled in a little town with the funny name of Doraville in the state of Georgia.

He was born at the local hospital one year later and lived all of his life in the same area where his parents settled in, Dad getting a job at the Ford plant and Mum cleaning houses. Over the years, they scraped up enough for a down payment on a small two-bedroom house. They were happy even though it was a struggle and Frankie knew this early in life and when he got into high school, Frankie got himself a part-time job and stuck to it all the way into his university days saving for study and help his parents out when things were tight.

Frankie, while in his freshman year at Georgia State University, studying and hoping to get a degree in accounting, continues the same job he had while in high school. He enjoyed his job and made some money while he worked at Zesto's, a sloppy burger joint that folks knew the fat and grease in the burgers was terrible for their health but it was made Zesto's, well Zesto's so tasty, and customers kept coming for more and did not care if they later died from it.

Life was good for Frankie and his parents until the day of the car accident. His parents were driving from church one morning and a car ran a stop sign and hit Frankie parent's car, killing them instantly.

With no life insurance, no credit insurance on the mortgage and little savings Frankie had no choice but to sell the house, pay off the balance on the mortgage and take the little money he had left over from the sale and restart his life; this time on his own.

He was fortunate that while in the student centre in the morning; he saw an ad for a roommate in Doraville. Frankie checked it out, spoke with the landlady and then the house's current occupants and was accepted by both into the group housing.

The house was owned by a Miss Marshall who turned out to be a spinster with plenty of money but a heart of gold. Miss Marshall rented out the four-bedroom house with two bathrooms and only charged minimal rent of $400 a month, including all the utilities. All the roommates had to agree to, in writing, was to pay the rent and do the assigned chores each had, which, in Frankie's case, became mowing the lawn.

The new roommates composed of Marcelo (working on a Business Administration degree and responsible for all minor handy work in the house), Pablo (also a Business Administration degree candidate and he was in charge of all kitchen duties) and Marisol (Bachelor of Science with a concentration in biology) which Marisol hoped would help her advance into a medical degree and her responsibility was making sure the house was tidy and clean.

Frankie inherited his chore when the previous roommate who had recently graduated from university and left the house, hence the room availability. Frankie did not mind a little work if it kept the rent down. He spent his time between class, studying, working at Zesto's, mowing the lawn, and hanging out with his new roommates.

Starting his sophomore year, everything was going great for Frankie. He got along wonderfully with his other three roommates, each doing their chores and the house was pretty well organised, clean, and cosy but he had an issue which he kept to himself. His attraction to Marisol.

At first, he thought little of it. Marisol was nice to everyone in the house.

When they had a party, she acted as the chief host and ensured everyone had a great time. She danced with everyone that came to the event and paid no particular attention to anyone.

Frankie fell for her hard but did nothing to show he had feelings. He did not want to make a fool of himself and then breakup a wonderful friendship if Marisol was not interested in him.

Yes, she paid attention to him by calling him to remind him to do the lawn, by serving him dishing out a plate of vegetables or something when the roommates had lunch or dinner together or by making sure he never wore a dirty shirt always dusting him off but then again, she did the same for Marcelo and Pablo.

Marisol was just nice, and he was sure she was not interested in him in the same way he was interested in her because she never told him, so for the entire four years together, he never acted on his feelings until this evening when his thoughts drifted and concentrated on Marisol.

When he first met Marisol, he got to know her quickly. She is intelligent, funny and she had a kindness in her he wished he could muster for himself as a virtue. Marisol was cheerful; her personality made the house into a home, and her smile brought a ray of cheerfulness into any room she entered.

Marisol was also a straight talker, letting you know exactly what she felt. Whether is it was politics (conservative), religion (agnostic), the weather (always nice, no matter how cold it got, or wet and miserable), you always knew where she stood and never made you feel bad or awkward if you disagree with her.

Live and let live was her motto, Frankie thought.

Her laugh was the key.

Frankie thought either Marisol was too kind and always laughed at his jokes or that maybe he should go to Las Vegas and try out for a stand-up comic.

For almost four years, Frankie lived in the same house with Marisol, seeing her, smelling her, hearing her laugh and not once did he approach her to go on a date. Yes, they went out, but as a group. To basketball games, to a student convention or a student get together, even student rallies but never on an official date.

Frankie could not take his mind away from her as he laid in bed. Living in close quarters with others gave Frankie a perspective he never had as an only child. Marcelo and Pablo Frankie figured out early in his interview that they were gay but seemed like great guys and Frankie did not care which team they played on as long as they were good roommates to him and Frankie came to think of them over the years as a family.

As much as he liked Marcelo and Pablo, he never confined them to his feelings for Marisol. Maybe he should have done so the moment he started having feelings. Hindsight is always better sight, he thought.

Frankie looked at his alarm clock: 5:19 AM.

He must have been awake for over two hours, staring at the ceiling and thinking of Marisol. 'I need to do something about this,' thought Frankie. What exactly, he did not know.

Should he ask her out on a date? No, they are in their last semester and each would go their separate ways. She will think it is a friend's goodbye dinner.

Maybe confine with both Marcelo and Pablo and see if they can provide some advice? Duh, he thought, should have done that three years ago.

These four years together Frankie and Marisol had comforted one another through tragedies and triumph but never openly admit how they feel about each other, but Frankie never knew if she had feeling for him. He did not see any signs from her to that matter.

His gut feeling said he needed to do something, but what?

Should he just tell her how he felt? If he did not choose the right approach, he would look like an idiot, which he was many times, but if he did nothing, then he would never know.

Time was running out for Frankie. After May Marisol and he and the others would graduate, leaving poor Miss Marshall with the tasks of finding four new housemates. All Frankie could think was: We are all going our separate ways soon.

'That's it. I need to do something. Today, this morning, right now,' he whispered to himself.

Frankie goes into the bathroom and takes a long shower. He then does a meticulous shave, making sure not one stubble would show. He wanted this morning to look his best.

Returning to his room, his beautification continues with a quick clipping of his nails on both hands and feet. Why the feet? Thought Frankie to himself. He did not know, but it seemed to be a good idea.

A quick check in his closet finds his favourite Nautica polo shirt, and he lays it on his unmade bed. Then the khaki chinos and his brown moccasins and he gets ready to go downstairs.

One last look in the mirror and he goes downstairs and hears voices in the kitchen and as he goes in, he sees his roommates having breakfast at the table.

'Good morning, Frankie, my, you look spiffy this morning! What's up?' says Marcelo.

'Special day, my friend. Can I speak with you, Marisol?'

Marisol takes the last spoonful of Corn Flakes into her mouth, chews them down and gets up to take the bowl to the dishwasher: 'Of course, Frankie. What can I do for you?'

Frankie's instincts take hold of him at that moment and without thinking or hesitating, he holds Marisol's face in the cup of his hands and places the softest kiss he has ever done on Marisol's lips; he steps back and waits.

Pablo and Marcelo just stare at Marisol, then at Frankie and back to Marisol. The world seems to have stopped spinning.

After what seemed like an eternity, Frankie says: 'Marisol, I have been in love with you for the last four years and I could not express my feelings to you. Last night I could not sleep knowing that I might never see you again after this semester. I could not let you leave without letting you know how I felt. I know I sprung this on you and probably never gave you a hint of how I felt, but it is what it is and here I am asking you how you feel about me.'

Marisol continues to stand in front of Frankie holding the empty bowl.

Pablo and Marcelo scoot their chairs closer to Marisol and Frankie.

'Four years! You waited four years to tell me how you felt! What about my four years of giving you hint after hint about how I felt about you? You never acted on my hints and now you spring this on me and expect an answer?'

'Hints? What hints?'

Pablo and Marcelo scoot their chairs even closer to Marisol and Frankie. 'This is better than a tele-novella, Marcelo,' says Pablo. 'Shush, it's going to get better. I bet you' was Marcelo's response.

'What hints you ask, Frankie? Well, where do I start? OK, how about the number of times we had a group meal, and I stood close to you and served you either mashed potatoes, green beans, or anything and kept asking if it was enough? Or how about the many times I called you to ask if you were coming home to mow the lawn and you said you did it the week before and I acted like I did not know and persisted you come home and do the lawn, anyway. Add to this the time frequent times I brushed off imaginary dust or hairs or anything from your shoulders just to be close to you and touch you? How about I never introduced you to any of my girlfriends at all the parties we had here? You never thought that was strange? Do I need to go on, Frankie? Do I?'

It was Frankie's turn to stand there, mouth open and speechless.

'Oh, I love drama, Pablo. You are right. This scene is much better than a tele-novella.'

'Marisol, I, I…'

'What Frankie? I, I… doesn't tell me anything. What do you have to say?'

Once again, Frankie cups Marisol's face in his hand and kisses her and he steps back once more.

A long double sigh emits from Marcelo and Pablo.

'OK,' says Marisol, 'I accept your apology,' as she reaches up, cups Frankie's face in her hands, and kisses him.

'Oh yes Pablo you are right; this is better than a tele-novella,' says Marcelo.

ABOUT THE AUTHOR

José F. Nodar was born in La Habana, Cuba.

He grew up in a middle-class neighbourhood until the Cuban Revolution of 1959 threw a spanner into his happy life.

His parents heard a story that children under the age of eleven were to be sent to Russia for 'indoctrination.' This rumour was untrue, but I believed it to have been incited by the Catholic Archdiocese of Miami and the American Central Intelligence Agency under the title 'The Pedro Pan Project' or 'The Peter Pan Project.'

This led José to be one of the 14,000 children sent to the USA to disrupt Fidel Castro's regime, but it disrupted the lives of so many families instead.

In 1968 José's parents left Cuba under the 'Freedom Flights' (known in Spanish as Los Vuelos de la Libertad) and these flights transported about Cubans to Miami twice daily, five times per week from 1965 to 1973 and José and his parents reunited after all those years.

From 1968 to 1970, José and his parents lived and worked in San Juan, Puerto Rico where they owned a restaurant, but this type of work proved unsatisfactory to José, and he headed back north to Atlanta, Georgia where he had some friends and a possibility of a new job career.

This job career turned out to be in the banking arena and then into international consulting, which became the backbone of his professional life.

In 2008 the Great Financial Crisis (GFC) struck the financial world José and his Australian wife (Miriam) moved to Australia and pursue their lives there.

In 2014, José and Miriam retired in Spring Farm, New South Wales (a Sydney suburb) and have enjoyed their retirement ever since while pursuing their hobbies and interests.

José Nodar © 2022

www.ingramcontent.com/pod-product-compliance
Lightning Source LLC
Chambersburg PA
CBHW072359110726
47909CB00003B/748